LIFE OF DAVID HOCKNEY

ALSO BY CATHERINE CUSSET

*No Tomorrow: The Ethics of Pleasure
in the French Enlightenment*

The Story of Jane

LIFE OF
DAVID HOCKNEY

A Novel

Catherine Cusset

Translated from the French by
Teresa Lavender Fagan

OTHER PRESS/NEW YORK

Copyright © Éditions Gallimard, 2018
Originally published in 2018 as *Vie de David Hockney:*
Roman by Éditions Gallimard, Paris

English translation copyright © Other Press, 2019

Poetry excerpts on pages 82–83 from "The Man with the Blue Guitar,"
by Wallace Stevens, 1937.

Production editor: Yvonne E. Cárdenas
Text designer: Jennifer Daddio / Bookmark Design & Media Inc.
This book was set in Goudy Oldstyle and Bernhard Gothic
by Alpha Design & Composition of Pittsfield, NH

1 3 5 7 9 10 8 6 4 2

Library of Congress Cataloging-in-Publication Data

Names: Cusset, Catherine, 1963- author. | Fagan, Teresa Lavender, translator. |
Translation of: Cusset, Catherine, 1963- Vie de David Hockney.
Title: Life of David Hockney : a novel / Catherine Cusset ; translated by Teresa Fagan.
Other titles: Vie de David Hockney. English
Description: New York : Other Press, 2019. | "Originally published in 2018 as
Vie de David Hockney: Roman by Éditions Gallimard, Paris."
Identifiers: LCCN 2018045824 (print) | LCCN 2018046618 (ebook) |
ISBN 9781590519844 (ebook) | ISBN 9781590519837 (paperback)
Subjects: LCSH: Hockney, David--Fiction. | BISAC: FICTION / Biographical. |
FICTION / Gay.
Classification: LCC PQ2663.U84 (ebook) | LCC PQ2663.U84 V5413 2019 (print) |
DDC 843/.914—dc23
LC record available at https://lccn.loc.gov/2018045824

LIFE OF DAVID HOCKNEY

THE RABBIT AND THE MAGPIE

This is a novel. All facts are true, but I have imagined feelings, thoughts, and dialogue. I used intuition and deduction rather than actual invention. I sought coherence and connected pieces of Hockney's life puzzle from what I found in many sources—autobiographies, biographies, interviews, essays, films, and articles. This portrait reflects my vision of David Hockney, even if it was he, his work, his words that inspired me. I hope the artist will consider this an homage.

Why Hockney? It may seem odd to take hold of the life of someone alive and create a novel. But it is he who took hold of me. When I read about him, something happened. He started to live in my head like a character in a novel. We had in common a double life between Europe and the United States. His freedom fascinated me. I felt like transforming all the documentary material into a narrative that would shed light on his journey from the inside by focusing on the links between love, creation, life, and death.

I met him for the first time in May 2018, in New York, four months after sending him a copy of my novel in French. At lunch I mentioned how a visit to Holland Park in London had made me understand the turning point in his painting in 2002.

"Yes," David said. "That was the first spring I saw in twenty years."

I knew that, I had read about it.

He continued: "One day, as I sat on a bench, smoking a cigarette, I saw a black rabbit. Then a magpie landed next to him. I was watching the rabbit and the black-and-white bird when these three girls jogging through the park passed by me. One of them brought her hand to her lips, gesturing, *No!* She was thinking, *What a horrible old man, smoking in the park!* These girls didn't see the rabbit and the magpie. They didn't look at the park. They only cared about their bodies."

"That's a great story," I said. "I wish I had put it in my novel!"

So here it is, as a bonus for my American readers.

ONE

A TALL BLOND MAN
IN A WHITE SUIT

His father was a pacifist. He had seen what World War I had done to his older brother, who had been gassed and returned home destroyed, a ghost. In '39 he protested against the new war. He lost his job, any government assistance, earned many enemies, and was shunned by his neighbors. "Children, don't be concerned with what the neighbors think." This was the big life lesson he taught his four sons and one daughter.

Ken didn't have much money, but was very resourceful. He would retrieve old, broken prams that had been discarded and would repair, paint, and sell them as new. After the war he did the same with bicycles. When he was little, David found nothing more beautiful than the moment when the paintbrush in his father's hand made contact with the frame of a bicycle. The rusty metal became bright red, in just a second, like magic. The world had changed color.

David was proud of his father. A true artist, his mother would say, frowning. Ken was so clever that he dressed elegantly without spending a penny. He would attach to his collars or ties paper that he decorated with dots and stripes in bright colors. David admired his creativity. After restoring a bike, Ken would put an ad in the local newspaper with the number of the phone in the booth next to their house, carry an armchair into the street, and settle down comfortably with his newspaper, holding an umbrella when it rained: that was his shop. The day he decided to redecorate the house, he nailed boards onto the doors and painted sunsets on them. The young boy never tired of looking at them.

David had a vague memory of planes flying above their heads and of the day when he had been evacuated from their home with his two brothers, his older sister, and his mother, who was nine months' pregnant, but not of the terror of his older brother, who gripped their mother's hand, almost crushing it, during the bombings—"please, Mum, pray for us"—nor of the bomb that had destroyed several houses on their street and shattered the windows of all those that had remained standing, except theirs. His childhood was filled with games played outside with his brothers and sister, with hiking in the woods, riding bikes on the country roads, Sunday school—spent drawing what they had learned that day at services: Jesus walking on the water, Jesus resuscitating the dead—and Boy Scout camps where he kept the logbook by illustrating their activities. On Saturdays, his father would take them to the movies to see Superman, Charlie Chaplin, or Laurel and Hardy. Ken bought seats for sixpence, the cheapest, those in the first three rows, and the screen was so close that David felt he was actually in the film. For Christmas they would go to the Alhambra, where the pantomimes made them cry laughing. On Sunday they could invite their friends over for tea, which his mother prepared. A delicious odor of cake that had just come out of the oven filled the house, the table was covered with brioches, mini-sandwiches, and jams, and the kitchen was filled with the sound of children laughing, allowed to help themselves to as much as they wanted, four, five, or six slices of cake.

David didn't even know they were poor. His greatest pleasure didn't cost a thing: to board a bus (free), climb the stairs to the upper level, and find a seat in the front next to a man who blew cigarette smoke into his face, or an old lady whose shopping bag he asked her to move, excusing himself politely. He watched out of the huge window as the street and the landscape in the distance passed by. When he was a teenager he felt the same pleasure when he pushed his bike to the top of Garrowby Hill on the country road near the farm where he worked for two summers in a row: from atop the hill he could see the entire York Valley, a panorama of 360 degrees without an obstacle. What could be more beautiful?

He wanted for nothing, except paper. For a boy who loved to draw as much as he did, the scarcity of paper after the war was a problem. He filled the margins of anything he could find: books, school notebooks, newspapers, comic strips. Sometimes one of his brothers would shout at him, furious: "You've scribbled in the speech bubble again! Now we can't read what it says!" Could one spend one's life drawing? Yes, if one was an artist. What was an artist? Someone who created Christmas cards or movie posters. There were forty movie theaters in their city and posters everywhere. David studied attentively the man leaning over a woman with a sunset in the background: he thought he could do as well, if not better. And in the evenings, or on a Sunday after church, he could draw what he wanted, just for himself. After paying the bills, with a bit of luck, he would still have enough money to buy some paper. It would be a nice life.

Little David dreamed.

He was not just a dreamer, but also a good student. He received a scholarship to go to the best school in the city. He was well liked at school because he was funny and everyone loved his drawings. When his friends asked him for a poster for their club, David never said no. Those works were displayed on a board at the school entrance, which had become his own private exhibition space. They were often stolen, which didn't bother him. In class, he drew instead of taking notes. The day when his English teacher asked him to read his essay out loud and he responded that he hadn't written it, but had "done this," showing an elaborate collage, a self-portrait that he had spent the hour making, there was a moment of dramatic suspense in the class before the teacher said, "But that's marvelous, David!"

His was a happy childhood. Of course, he fought with his brothers, argued with his friends, and was occasionally unjustly punished. But any resentment never lasted. Up to the age of fourteen he never knew how ignorant the world could be.

He was almost fourteen when the headmaster of his school wrote to his parents recommending that they send their son to an art school. Even if David was perfectly capable of studying the humanities in a regular high school, it was clear that drawing was his passion and his talent. He was incredibly grateful to the headmaster who had understood him so well, and to his parents who loved him enough to agree to his transfer to a professional, thus less prestigious, school. They arranged an interview at the Bradford School of Art, he showed his drawings, and he was accepted. Since he was a scholarship student, he just had to obtain the approval of the city's department of education to complete his enrollment. The response came a month later: "After careful consideration the Committee has concluded that your son's best interests would be served by completion of his course of general education before specializing in art."

There was no getting around it. David had to go to the high school he had been assigned, and for two years study math, English, history, geography, French, and chemistry from morning to night. No art courses, of course. His parents tried to console him: two years will go by quickly, they said. David had never felt such rage. For the bureaucrat who had signed that letter, two years were nothing more than the two seconds it had taken for him to scrawl his signature. What gave that man whom he had never met the right to decide his life? He would show that fascist what he was capable of. He stopped working. His grades plummeted, he was repeatedly warned. He didn't care. He would be expelled and would lose his scholarship. A terrible waste, his teachers said. Great. But an angel was watching over him. His mother, who didn't try to reason with him, quietly intervened. She went out and knocked on the door of one of their neighbors, who taught at the Bradford School of Art, and asked him if he might give free lessons to their son. The boy was gifted, and the teacher agreed. The weekly evening classes provided the oxygen David needed to breathe, and his grades improved.

In the afternoons, he sometimes went to the movies instead of doing his homework. He had found a way of getting in for free. He would stand outside next to the exit door and, as soon as someone opened the door, he would walk inside backward, making it look as if he was coming out. One afternoon, when he was absorbed in an American film noir with Humphrey Bogart, he didn't notice the individual who sat down next to him in the almost empty theater. In the dark, a hand took his and placed it on something warm, hard, and hairy. David's heart was beating incredibly fast. He was afraid, but didn't resist. The hand that covered his moved it up and down faster and faster until the man groaned softly. He left the theater before the end of the film. When David went out, his cheeks were on fire, his fingers were sticky, he couldn't stop thinking of what had just happened. So fear wasn't incompatible with pleasure? It had been the most exciting thing that had ever happened to him, and he couldn't say anything about it to his mother. Could something that made you feel so good be bad? His friends were always talking about girls. He'd never experienced such a thrill with any girl.

He turned sixteen and was done with high school. None of his older brothers or his sister had gone to university. His brother Paul, who also liked to draw, would have liked to study graphic art, but when he graduated, he had to take a job as a clerk in an office. So it would have been unfair for his younger sibling to go to the School of Art. "Why don't you look for a job in a commercial art company in Leeds?" his mother asked him. David put together a portfolio of his drawings, got on his bike, and went off to show it to possible employers whose responses he was happy to bring back home: "You must begin by learning the basics, my boy." The day when one of them offered him an unpaid internship during which he would be trained, and which guaranteed him a job at the end, David answered that he would think about it. He didn't tell his mother.

She ended up giving in. She wrote to the Bradford department of education on his behalf, and it granted him a scholarship of thirty-five pounds. It wasn't much, but his brother was earning scarcely twice that at a job where he was dying of boredom. David spent the summer on a farm tying together and storing ears of corn, and had a deep tan when he started at the Bradford School of Art in September, in the new outfit he had bought at the thrift store with his father. With his long red scarf, his striped suit with trousers that were too short, and a round hat on his black hair, he looked like a Russian peasant. His friends nicknamed him Boris.

They could tease him and call him what they liked, and he was ready to laugh along. Nothing bothered him. After waiting for two years, he was finally free to indulge his passion from morning to night. The school had two departments, painting and graphic art. When the director asked him to choose between the two, he immediately said: "I want to be an artist." "Do you have private income, David?" the director asked him, visibly surprised. Not understanding what he meant, David couldn't answer. "You'll go into the graphic art department, my friend," the man concluded, believing he was doing him a favor. That was the commercial branch of the school, and it guaranteed that students would earn a decent living following the completion of their studies. After two weeks, David asked to be transferred. "Then you should be trained to teach," he was told. Whatever they wanted, as long as they let him paint.

The old neighbor who had given him private lessons the year before had warned him of the danger that threatened students at the art school—idleness. David worked twelve hours a day. He wanted to learn everything. Anatomy, perspective, drawing, engraving, oil painting, copying out of books or from nature. His instructors' comments on his work delighted him because they saw things he hadn't noticed, expanded and deepened his vision. A young professor, Derek Stafford, taught him that drawing wasn't just an imitation, but a cerebral act. You have to think, move, change your perspective, view the object from several angles. David had never met anyone as intelligent and sophisticated as Derek. He wasn't from Bradford. The war had interrupted his studies at the best art school, the Royal College of Art in London. He had traveled in France and Italy, had read everything. He invited students over to his place, offered them cigarettes, French wine, and let them vomit in his bathroom. He told them to go to London, it was essential for their education. At eighteen, David went to London for the first time with some friends he had met at the School of Art. They hitchhiked at night, arrived in the big city at dawn, bought tickets for the Circle Line, and slept in the subway until the museums opened. He saw more art in one day than he had seen since he was born. He discovered Francis Bacon, Dubuffet. And Picasso. At the Bradford School of Art there was a student they called Picasso because he didn't know how to draw. David shook his head; they were wrong, the man definitely knew how to draw!

After two years at the art school, David was bold enough to propose two paintings to the Leeds art gallery for the biennial exhibition of Yorkshire artists. He figured the worst that could happen was he would be refused. To his surprise, his pictures were accepted. So you just had to dare, to go beyond what was normally done or not done, and things happened. He didn't have the indecency to put a price on his paintings—he was just a student. At the exhibition opening, where they served sandwiches and tea for free, he felt the joy of legitimately belonging in this gallery where his work was exhibited alongside that of other artists. He was only eighteen and he was one of them. He had invited his parents. Their pride at seeing their son's two works hanging next to those of his teachers swelled his own. Shortly after they left, a man came up to David and offered him ten pounds for the portrait of his father. Ten pounds! More than a quarter of his scholarship, enough to live on for three months, for something he'd done for pleasure? As he opened his mouth to say yes he realized that the painting didn't belong to him. His father had paid for the canvas, he had only made the marks on it. "Just a moment!" He ran off to phone his father, who was happy to learn that someone wanted to buy his portrait despite the muddy color his son had applied to his face against his best advice, under the pretext that that's how they painted at the School of Art. With the ten pounds in his pocket, David still couldn't believe it, and called his mother: "Mum, I just sold Dad!" She started laughing. He celebrated the event by inviting his friends to the pub that very evening. The party cost him a pound, an extravagance, but he still had nine left to buy paint and canvases.

Derek and London had expanded his thinking. He had understood that you couldn't become an artist if you stayed in Bradford. He had to go to London, study in an art school worthy of the name. He spent two summers in a row painting outside in the streets of Bradford, transporting his paint and brushes in a pram that his father had repaired. He begged his mother to let him use a room in the house as a studio. She got mad when he spilled paint on the floor or didn't put the caps on his tubes, she criticized his negligence, his lack of respect for others, but he knew that she would say yes—she was on his side. In the spring of '57, when David wasn't yet twenty, his portfolio was ready. He sent it to the Royal College of Art in London, as well as to another art school, the Slade, to increase his enrollment chances, because the Royal College took only one student out of ten. He was chosen for an interview and went to London, unable to sleep the night before, aware of his ignorance and his inferiority compared to his rivals, who had grown up surrounded by museums.

He was accepted.

Before starting at the school, David had to fulfill his military service requirement. A conscientious objector, like his father, he was sent to a hospital as a health care aide, first in Leeds, then in Hastings, and he spent two years taking care of elderly and sick patients all day long, rubbing their decrepit bodies with ointment, and washing the dead. He didn't have time to paint, or even to think. He fell asleep at night trying to read Proust and wondering what an asparagus was. He was aware of his good fortune. He wouldn't be doing this exhausting and thankless work his entire life. The Royal College awaited him.

The time finally arrived.

He was in London, in the most prestigious art school in England, one of the best in the world. His new friends were filled with certainty on subjects he had never even thought about. The day when one of them exclaimed, "You can't paint like Monet anymore after Pollock!" David blushed as if they were talking about him. He discovered that figure painting belonged to the past, that it was antimodern.

French painting was of no interest to any of the other students. He would have been ashamed to show them the portrait of his father that he had been so proud to sell four years earlier, and which he had painted in the vein of the Euston Road School or of French artists such as Vuillard and Bonnard. People were interested only in American abstract works: huge paintings that represented nothing, whose titles were numbers. David had, of course, seen the big exhibition of abstract expressionism at the Tate Gallery in the winter of '59 and discovered de Kooning, Pollock, Rothko, Sam Francis, and Barnett Newman. That exhibition, then those at the Whitechapel Gallery, had shaken his conception of art. You were contemporary or you were nothing.

What would his first work at the school be? Certainly not a figurative painting. He already had a strong Yorkshire accent, he was terrified at the idea that he would be considered provincial, a Sunday painter. He had to stay on safe ground: drawing. A human skeleton hanging in one of the rooms inspired him. A skeleton, that was original. A large drawing with all the details would reveal his perfect training in anatomy and perspective.

Everyone noticed his skeleton. A tour de force, they said. He had passed his first trial, hadn't made a fool of himself. He felt a bit more at ease. One of his friends even offered him five pounds for it. He was an American, a rich student, a former GI who had returned to London on a generous GI Bill stipend. You had to be American to pay five pounds for a student's drawing. Ron was five years older than he, married, and had a baby. He lived in a real house, unlike David, who shared a tiny room with another student in the lively Earl's Court neighborhood. Ron painted slowly and didn't care what the others thought. His free spirit reminded David of his stubborn father. They became friends. They both arrived at school early in the morning, earlier than the other students, and had a cup of tea together before getting to work. They talked about art, art history, contemporary art. David had realized for some time that the painters he had known in Bradford, even his teachers at the School of Art, weren't artists. He finally understood why: they didn't question their place and relevance in the history of art. One couldn't be an artist without asking oneself that fundamental question and finding an answer to it. He no longer had anything in common with the innocent boy he had been, the one who spent happy summers ambling around, pushing his pram filled with tubes of paint and brushes, stopping here and there to sketch a tree or a house. Figure painting was good for poster and Christmas card artists. He had had a close call, but the new atmosphere he was breathing in had opened his eyes: he would be modern. Ron shook his head and smiled.

David should have been happy. He had done everything he could to get into this school. The day he was accepted, he had felt as if he had passed through the eye of a needle, had entered paradise, had been rescued from the life of an office employee that was the lot of his brothers, his sister, and his neighbors in Bradford. During the two years he had worked at the hospital, he had dreamt of his future existence and developed a serene patience, knowing that his deliverance would come and awaken him from what felt like a century of sleep. Now he was finally free, but that anticipated, desired happiness that should have been within his grasp escaped him. For the first time, he no longer felt joy in painting. He felt strangely detached from his work, without energy or enthusiasm. Maybe he had been wrong. Maybe he was just an impostor. His American friend listened to the twenty-two-year-old, completely at a loss, pour out his anxieties. They also talked about other things, politics, literature, friendship, love, the vegetarian diet that David, like his parents, practiced. His daily conversations with Ron at least allowed him to feel less alone.

"This is what you should paint," Ron said one day. "Things that matter to you. You don't have to worry about being contemporary. You already are, since you live in your time."

The idea was interesting. There was no point in struggling to belong to one's time—one belonged to it by definition. Ron's figures, indeed, didn't seem to have been painted in Manet's or Renoir's time. In any case, something had to change. If David didn't rediscover pleasure in painting, he would end up like an old, dried-up lemon left out on a kitchen counter. As a matter of fact, he felt like painting vegetables. No one could accuse him of being antimodern, because their round shapes seemed respectfully abstract. But in his mind, they were vegetables. He then painted the can of Typhoo Tea from which he took a bag every morning when he arrived at school, and which reminded him of his mother. In addition to the words "Typhoo Tea," he had the idea of adding a letter or a number here and there which would force the viewer to get closer to the painting to decipher them. He was smuggling in a bit of intimacy. The letters and numbers engaged the viewer instead of leaving him at a distance, as abstract painting did.

Ron shared a corner of his studio down the hall with another student, and when David went to see him in the afternoon, he also chatted with his studio mate. Adrian was gay. The first openly gay man David, at the age of twenty-two, had ever met. He had known for a long time that he liked men, but his sexual activity was limited to rare, furtive encounters about which he spoke to no one in places where he went alone. The day when one of his friends told him, "I saw you in that pub with that bloke and I saw what you were doing!" he had blushed, terribly embarrassed by the unfortunate coincidence that had brought a student he knew into a pub far away from their school, where a stranger he had met an hour earlier in the Leicester Square movie theater was fondling him. Afterward, his own reaction had made him angry. Would he have blushed if the student had caught him with a girl? And would the student have even mentioned it? What gave him the right to talk to him with such mocking familiarity? David painted a work that he called *Shame*, without any other identifiable shape than that of an erect penis in the foreground. While he listened to Adrian unashamedly tell him about his homosexual adventures, he thought, *That's how I want to live.* Adrian advised him to read the American poet Walt Whitman, whom David had heard of, and the Egyptian Greek poet Constantine Cavafy, whom he hadn't.

The summer he turned twenty-three, he read Whitman and Cavafy. Whitman's poetry was easy to find, but not Cavafy's. At the public library in Bradford his works weren't on the shelves; you had to get them from a special room, the library's "Inferno." When he was checking the book out, the library employee gave him a suspicious look, one that implied that the prodigal son who had gone to live in London had obviously been debauched, and was about to read this book holding it in one hand, using the other to rid himself of the tension that reading it would cause. At the end of the summer, he couldn't bring himself to return it. It wasn't just the dread of again confronting the frown of the librarian. He simply couldn't separate himself from Cavafy—the book belonged to him.

He immediately fell in love with the Greek poet's humor. One of his favorite poems was "Waiting for the Barbarians," with its refrain "The barbarians are coming today," and its final verse that revealed the absence of the barbarians whose arrival was so feared: "Those people were a sort of solution." How true that was, and how we were always seeking hypocritical pretexts! People were so lacking in courage and freedom! The two poets, the American and the Greek, expressed everything he was feeling in simple words that he could understand, unlike Proust, whose meaning escaped him. "And his arm lay lightly around my breast—and that night I was happy," wrote Whitman, talking about the love between two men. For the first time in a year, David no longer had any doubt: he had to paint what mattered to him. He had just turned twenty-three. There was nothing more important than desire and love. He had to find a way to represent what was forbidden in images, just as Whitman and Cavafy had done through words. No one could authorize him to do it—no professor, no other artist. It had to be his decision, his creation, the exercise of his freedom.

Having returned to the Royal College, he produced a series of paintings in which he slipped in words and even lines, some of which came from Walt Whitman, such as "We two boys together clinging," and others from graffiti he had read on the men's room door in the Earl's Court Tube station, such as "Ring me at…" or "My brother is only seventeen." Geometrical shapes like those in children's drawings, the figures were identifiable thanks to the hair, mouths, teeth, impish ears, and erect penises. To represent himself in these paintings, he borrowed a childlike code from Whitman that consisted of replacing the letters of the alphabet with numbers, drawing on the canvas in tiny script the numbers "4.8" which represented his initials, and the numbers "23.23" for Walt Whitman. These were so small, so light, that one could choose not to see them and to interpret David's new works in a purely artistic context by seeing the influence of Pollock or Dubuffet in them. His professors were in the dark (so to speak). It was an excellent way to dupe the system.

He no longer felt the gloomy lack of inspiration he had felt the year before, and didn't stop painting, completing one work after another. He had established a routine: he arrived early, when there was still no one at the school except Ron, and he painted in blissful quiet for two hours before the others arrived. Around 3:00 p.m., when his fellow students left their easels for some tea, David slipped away and went to the movies, alone or with the girlfriend of one of his friends, Ann, a pretty, red-headed student who loved American films as much as he did. He returned to the college just as the students were leaving, and he worked late into the night, in peace. In any event, he really had nowhere to go. He had moved out of the tiny room he had been sharing, and was now living, at the same price, in a shed in the yard behind the house. He was delighted to be alone, but the comforts of the place were so rudimentary that he couldn't do anything but sleep there.

A new student had arrived in September, Mark, an American as openly gay as Adrian, who had brought from America something that David was quick to borrow: magazines filled with photos of young, blond, muscular men in their underwear, which revealed more than it hid. While thumbing through them and getting excited by the photos, David wondered again why something so beautiful, which elicited such pleasure, should be hidden. These magazines were printed in the United States. Two of his three closest friends at the RCA were American. He had never encountered a homosexual in the town where he had grown up, and any sexual relationship between two consenting adult men was considered a crime by the British penal code. The young blond men who triumphantly showed off their biceps on the pages of *Physique Pictorial* made him want to immediately fly off to America. "If you come to New York one day, you're welcome to stay with me," Mark had told him, as if he could have taken a train to New York as easily as to Bradford. An airplane ticket no doubt cost hundreds or thousands of pounds. It was another universe. David had never been out of England.

He was grateful to Mark, Adrian, and Ron for that breath of freedom that they blew into his life. When he went home at Christmas or Easter, he was happy to see his parents and talk with his brothers and sister sitting around the good vegetarian meals their mother prepared. They asked about life in the big city, and David explained what American abstract expressionism was; he talked about the exhibition of Young Contemporary Artists for which critics had created the expression "Pop Art," and of the young art dealer who had really liked the four paintings he had exhibited in order to demonstrate his pictorial virtuosity. It was all very promising. But how could he have mentioned the photos in *Physique Pictorial*, the homosexuality of Mark and Adrian, the men he exchanged looks with in the subway toilets, or his desire to use painting to depict a reality about which he didn't have the right to speak? His oldest brother was married; the youngest was engaged. Neither of them asked him if he had a girlfriend. The subject never came up, as if an artist didn't have a body—rather, as if they knew, but didn't want to know.

And yet he had a body. And a heart.

One night at the Royal College, at the end of a party during which there had been a lot of drinking, one of his friends demonstrated a new dance called the cha-cha-cha. David watched him, rocking on his chair, and when Peter smiled and held out his hand for him to join him, that smile penetrated and suddenly irradiated him. It was like a bolt of lightning. It truly was a bolt, because he was stunned, his ears were ringing. He didn't want to dance. He preferred to watch. He asked for another demonstration, then another, without taking his eyes off the graceful body, the hips that turned to the right, to the left, and the sensual lips pursed as if to kiss, while the boy looked straight at him singing "cha-cha-cha." Peter was sexier than Marilyn, sexier than the living doll in the song by Cliff Richard that David liked so much. A boy doll. David would have given his kingdom for a kiss, but didn't ask for one, he was shy and polite, and above all he knew that Peter had a girlfriend. For months the vision of Peter dancing for him, his graceful hips and his puckered lips haunted him day and night. That's what he wanted to put into his paintings, that burning desire, his desire for Peter and for his body, a desire that split him in two, because there was sex on the one side and love on the other, and the two could not be reconciled. They could come together only when he was in front of his easel, and he felt alive and full of desire when he painted *The Cha Cha that was Danced in the Early Hours of 24th March, 1961*, depicting the movement of Peter's body, using bright red, blue, and yellow for the background and writing in tiny letters here and there "I love every movement," "penetrates deep down," "gives instant relief from." It wasn't a painting. It was life.

He had painted so much during the autumn that by winter he was like the grasshopper who had been singing all summer: he didn't have a penny left to buy canvases and paint. Luckily, the department of graphic art gave out materials for free. David didn't have a choice. But in his etchings, as in his paintings, he created what interested him, engraving visions inspired by the poetry of Walt Whitman or Constantine Cavafy. In April a friend offered to sell him for forty pounds a plane ticket to New York which the friend couldn't use. Forty pounds to fly to New York? That was an offer you couldn't refuse. He would find the money. He would work to pay his friend back.

That rainy day in April, he had ten shillings in his pocket—the last of his money—when he left his little shed behind the house in Earl's Court. It was pouring rain. A taxi was parked on the other side of the street. The taxi ride to the college would cost five shillings, half of what he had left, while the Tube, which wasn't far, would be only a few pence, but he would still have to walk ten minutes to get to the school. He felt an urge to do what so many Londoners did without a second thought: cross the street, open the taxi door, get into the rear of the cab, which was dry and comfortable, sit down on the padded seat, and say in a voice full of natural authority, "To the Royal College, please." And that's what he did.

At the school, a letter was waiting for him. When he tore open the envelope and took out the sheet of paper folded in thirds, another piece of paper fell out on the floor. He picked it up. It was a check for one hundred pounds made out to him. He frowned and reread the name, convinced he was imagining it. In the letter, a certain Mr. Erskine, whom he didn't know, congratulated him for the prize his etching *Three Kings and a Queen* had just won. David had indeed done an etching with that title, but he had never entered it into a competition. He was baffled. It was either a miracle or the gods were playing a joke on him. He had decided to spend the last of his money on a whim, without thinking of the future, and a good fairy was rewarding him by sending him two hundred times more than he had. Later that day he learned that the good fairy was a professor in the department of engraving who had found David's work on a shelf and had sent it to the jury without even asking him. But he shook his head. Quite obviously, it was thanks to that taxi.

Later that spring he sold a few paintings and prints. In July he boarded a plane for the first time. He was just twenty-four, with three hundred pounds to his name. He landed in New York, where Mark was waiting for him.

He had never experienced such heat and humidity; it was heavy, unbearable, and he sweat so much that his shirt was permanently glued to his skin. But it was the city he had dreamed of, luminous, noisy, vibrant, where you could buy beer or a newspaper at three in the morning. And there were so many gay bars! And so many vegetarian restaurants! So many museums, too, and of course he visited them all, but he hadn't come for that. It was for Times Square, Christopher Street, the East Village—the movie theaters, sex-shops, clubs, the piers on the banks of the Hudson where men weren't wearing shirts—all the decadence of a stifling summer. He stayed with Mark, whose parents had a house on Long Island, and met one of his friends, Ferrill, who became his lover. His first lover, whom he didn't have to hide. He now had two guides to introduce him to gay New York.

One afternoon at Mark's, a TV commercial caught their attention. There was a young woman with dyed, golden blond hair getting out of a plane and jumping into the arms of a man, another one playing pool, and yet another, running, a dog at her side, with a radiant smile, her hair flying in the wind, while a woman's voice asked, "Is it true blondes have more fun?" Then a male narrator interrupted the music: "Lady Clairol blond is a way to live. So have a little fun, lighten up and shine the Lady Clairol way!" The three young men, who loved the film *Some Like It Hot*, the obvious inspiration for the commercial, looked at each other.

Fifteen minutes later they came out of a drugstore with a bag containing the magic potion. Laughing, they read the instructions, mixed the solution in the bathroom, got undressed, and shampooed each other in the shower. The metamorphosis took place before their eyes. They became three tall peroxided blonds. They cried laughing, especially when Mark's father, who came back from work at the end of the afternoon, saw the three blond creatures sprawled out on the sofa, and almost had a heart attack. It was true: blondes really did have more fun.

David looked at himself in the mirror and couldn't believe his eyes. It was like the taxi in London. Magic.

You acted on a whim without thinking about the consequences, just for fun, and you won. That was the secret to life. He had just transformed himself into a blond like the models in *Physique Pictorial.* Up to then, he had considered himself neither handsome nor ugly—people told him he was "cute"—but suddenly he had become someone else, a man with striking blond hair, whom you couldn't help but notice. He liked his new hair color, not because "blondes have more fun," but because he had transformed himself. He was his own creation. He had been reborn. The color signaled his gay identity—his truest, most intimate self—and at the same time it was an artifice, a mask, a lie. Nature and artifice were thus not at odds, any more than were the figurative and abstraction, poetry and graffiti, quotes and originality, playing and reality. You could combine everything. Life, like painting, was a stage on which you played a role.

It was an extraordinary summer. He left Mark's parents' house—they had become tired of the eccentricities of their son's friends—and moved to Brooklyn, where Ferrill had a small, comfortable apartment with thick carpeting that swallowed your feet, a TV, and a real bathroom. David didn't know anyone that young who lived in such luxury. But the way Ferrill lived surprised him even more. You went into his place as through a revolving door. You took a shower with him, you slipped into his bed, then you left. Free love, without ties, without jealousy, without guilt. Just pleasure to give and receive. It was the life David yearned for. So long, Bradford! Even London seemed grim in comparison.

When he finally decided to contact the head of the department of prints at the Museum of Modern Art in New York, whose name Mr. Erskine had given him, another surprise awaited him. Not only did the man know who he was, and say he had been eager to meet him—he had received a letter from Erskine recommending his brilliant protégé—not only did he look at the etchings that David had brought from London, but he bought them! David couldn't believe it. He was still a student and MoMA in New York was acquiring his etchings. What generosity, and how easy life was in America!

The money came not a moment too soon, because he had run out. Now he could buy an American suit, one with a relaxed cut, light-colored, which was the height of fashion that summer. And a small transistor radio, to imitate the Americans who at first he thought were all deaf like his father, walking around with little devices in their ears, until Ferrill explained that they were simply wired day and night to music. A new man returned to London in September. A tall blond in a white suit. And he had brought back a few ideas with him. He was planning a very large painting, like those of the American abstract painters, so he would be given a very large space in the college studio; it wouldn't be an abstract painting, though, it would have figures. Inspired by Egyptian antiquities in the Metropolitan Museum, by Dubuffet, and by Cavafy's poem "Waiting for the Barbarians," he painted a procession of three people that he titled *A Grand Procession of Dignitaries in the Semi-Egyptian Style*, writing the title on the painting so it would be very clear that he wasn't taking himself seriously, and that it was all a game. A title that long had another advantage: since it took up several lines in the catalog of works exhibited at the college, it would be noticed. Clever like his father, David knew that success didn't just fall from the sky. In New York he had admired what in England would have been considered bad taste: the ease with which Americans knew how to sell themselves, without getting bogged down in false shame and feelings of guilt. After attracting the attention of critics, you had to hold on to it. A tall blond man in a white suit who didn't hide his deviant sexuality—that would intrigue them more than a painter from Bradford in West Yorkshire!

He was having a great time. He painted two figures top to tail, replacing their penises with tubes of Colgate toothpaste (dental hygiene was a real obsession in the United States), and titled the work *Cleaning Teeth, Early Evening (10 p.m.) W11*. It was completely obscene and very funny. In the print department he undertook his own version of *A Rake's Progress*, a series of engravings by the eighteenth-century painter William Hogarth, which show the downfall of a young man who lands in the big city and succumbs to vice. Referencing this classical work would enable David to recount his own New York adventures playfully: his arrival by plane, the sale of his etchings to the director of MoMA, the muscular Americans who jogged in Central Park in their sleeveless undershirts in front of the British weakling, the encounters among men in gay bars, the Clairol dye that changed the color of his hair and opened the doors to paradise, and even the ubiquitous little transistor radios all Americans were hooked up to, seemingly lacking any individuality...His perfect execution earned the praise of his professors.

Everything was going his way. He even had the nerve to tell the Royal College administrators that he didn't want the ugly, fat women in their forties who were sent to the students as models. Manet, Degas, and Renoir would never have become Manet, Degas, and Renoir if they hadn't been inspired by their models. He asked for a man, and the school, worn down by his insistence, ended up giving in. Since no one else wanted to paint a nude man, David hired for his own use, with the Royal College's money, a nice boy from Manchester he had just met. Mo introduced him to two of his friends, who soon became his own close friends, Ossie and Celia, who were studying fashion design. He had a fling with Ossie, a boy even wilder than he, who was also sleeping with Celia. Bisexual: another new concept. David was now living in London with the freedom he had discovered in New York. This was it, the bohemian life he had dreamed of ever since hearing the stories of Adrian and Mark: living with no fear of being who you are when you are different. Tolerance was the virtue of those whom social norms and moral reprobation had forced into hiding even when they weren't harming anyone.

He hadn't yet finished with school when the young art dealer Kasmin, who had admired his work the year before, offered him a contract. The dealer would give him six hundred pounds a year in exchange for the exclusive right to show his work, and more if his paintings sold. David couldn't believe his luck. All the other artists represented by Kasmin did abstract painting and were already known. He was the youngest and the only figurative painter. It had to be the effect of his blond hair and white suit. That summer, he didn't need his job delivering mail. He went to Italy with Jeff, an American Jewish boy he had met in New York. In the autumn, he was finally able to leave the shed in the back of the yard and move into an inexpensive one-bedroom on the ground floor of a building in Notting Hill, close to his friends Michael and Ann. Ossie and Celia soon joined them in the neighborhood. It was a seedy area—the house across the street had been converted to a nightclub and a brothel, and there was constantly blaring music coming out of it—but it was the first time that David had his own place to live, work, and listen to operas at full volume in the middle of London. And his best friends lived nearby. His apartment quickly became the center of their social life. His door was always open, people were coming and going—as at Ferrill's place in Brooklyn.

When he received a letter from the director of the Royal College informing him that his thesis on fauvism had been judged to be inadequate, and that he would there-fore not receive his diploma, he cursed angrily, then started laughing. It was a fact that he had done a half-assed job on that thesis, because he had had to get it in on time. In any event, Kasmin wasn't asking to see an official school document. Such was the world. On one side were the ad-ministrators, the narrow-minded who judged and quickly condemned, all those who were afraid to live; and on the other, art, instinct, desire, freedom, and faith in life. He was quite right to ignore those administrative hassles, since the director of the department of painting, who wanted to grant a gold medal to his best student and couldn't do it if he hadn't received his diploma, forced the college to reverse its decision. David didn't have anything against the medal; it impressed people and made his parents happy.

When a gallery owner who was organizing a group show asked the artists to reveal the source of their inspiration, he wrote: "I paint what I like when I like, and where I like."

Anything could be the subject of a painting: a poem, something one had seen, an idea, a feeling, a person. Really, anything. That was freedom. Derek had once told him to get rid of his clown image if he wanted his work to be taken seriously. But no: you could be both a clown and a serious painter!

The summer he turned twenty-six he returned to New York, this time on the *Queen Elizabeth*, to finish the etchings for *A Rake's Progress* and to see Jeff, the American he had traveled to Italy with the summer before. One afternoon, at Andy Warhol's apartment, where he had gone with his friend, he met a round, chubby-cheeked, bearded man who was the curator of contemporary art at the Metropolitan Museum, and the funniest, liveliest, most sardonic man he had ever encountered. They saw each other again the next day. Another gay Jewish man, of course, like all his American friends, but of European origin. Henry had emigrated with his parents from Brussels in 1940 in the last boat to the United States. David wasn't physically attracted to him, but had never felt so immediately close to anyone before. They talked back and forth, they finished each other's sentences, and couldn't stop laughing. They were about two years apart in age, liked the same poets, the same films, the same artists, the same books, and they had the same passion for opera. Across the Atlantic he had found his soulmate.

When he got back to London, a young man who had started a business selling prints made him an offer: he would print fifty series of the sixteen etchings of A Rake's Progress and would sell them for a hundred pounds each, which came to a total of five thousand pounds. It was the most money that David, or any other artist he knew, had ever made. Printing these series cost at most two or three pounds. There would be people who would pay a hundred for them? What madness! Of course, he wouldn't get all the money, because the dealer would take a percentage, as would Kasmin. But this was real money, and a sizable sum would be his. He could finally have a shower installed in his Notting Hill apartment to take long showers with his friends. This was only the beginning. Two London galleries would soon exhibit his works, and the Sunday Times of London planned to send him to Egypt at the newspaper's expense so he could bring back a notebook of sketches. And the money he earned with the series of etchings would enable him to fulfill a long-standing dream: to go to Los Angeles in January.

He suddenly saw in a flash the moment when the director of the Bradford School of Art asked him, "Do you have private income, David?" That image was immediately replaced by one of a fifteen-year-old boy trembling with fear and excitement while he jerked off a stranger in the darkness of a movie theater. He had come a long way since then.

TWO

SORROW LASTS THREE YEARS

David had just passed the exit sign for Cheyenne, heading toward Las Vegas. After driving for four days, stopping only to sleep in motels along the way, he was on the last leg of his trip. He was tired but liked the long hours spent driving west in his Triumph convertible listening to music, his head empty or full of thoughts, traveling through vast spaces. At sunset the sky, like a huge canvas, was covered in shades of orange and pink as bright and vibrant as neon signs. The roads were deserted, and David passed only a few rare trucks. It was the ideal speed for contemplating the purple of the mountains, the pink of the sky, and that immensity of emptiness all around him.

It would be his third teaching job. He wasn't afraid now the way he had been two years earlier when, on the road into Iowa at the end of June 1964, he had stopped at an optometrist's to buy a pair of enormous, thick, black frames to make himself look older and more professorial. That first experience had been a nightmare. Iowa City:

what a misnomer! When he got there after traveling for two days, he had gone through what looked like a suburb and found himself in the middle of cornfields: there had been no city. He had rarely been as bored as he had been for those six weeks. When Ossie had landed from London in the middle of August, he was waiting for him as if he were the Messiah. They had rushed off to New Orleans before driving to San Francisco through the big national parks. And he would not soon forget the YMCA in the Embarcadero in San Francisco. You just had to take a shower in the common bathroom in the middle of the night for boys to run out of the dormitories like shadows, but shadows with glorious bodies, to immediately offer whatever you wanted. You couldn't find such a paradise in Iowa City! Nor in Boulder, Colorado, where David had taught drawing courses in the summer of '65, although conditions had improved a bit: the mountain landscape was magnificent and he had had a fling with a very cute student. But, in such a gorgeous place, the university had given him a studio without a window, not even a little skylight! That was when he had painted his quite imaginary vision of the Rockies. At least he had understood that the Midwest wasn't for him.

It would be different at UCLA, where classes started on Monday. He imagined his future students: tall, muscular surfers, blond and tan, resembling the models in *Physique Pictorial*. They would be quite surprised to discover that the professor of the advanced painting course was so young and so cute. David planned to take full advantage of the respectful admiration completely lacking in irony that American students showed toward their professors. In addition, they were all smitten with the English accent, and that accent which in his own country betrayed his provincial and working-class origins here became an advantage, adding to his charm.

He listened to *The Magic Flute* and sang along at the top of his lungs while the sun sank below the horizon. After six months in London, he really missed the City of Angels. It had become his second home.

He was no longer the naive boy who had landed in L.A. in January '64, two and a half years earlier. Back then, on his second day, he had thought he would be able to conquer the city on a bike, since his legs alone, the day before, had taken him only as far as a gas station after walking for two hours from his motel! The distances didn't worry an Englishman who had spent his youth traveling around hilly Yorkshire on a bike. On a map he had seen that a long boulevard went straight from his motel on the Santa Monica beach to the heart of downtown L.A., to Pershing Square, where all the action in John Rechy's very sexy novel, *City of Night*, which had awakened intense fantasies in him, took place. Brimming with energy, he got on the bike he had bought that morning, a bit surprised all the same to discover that the boulevard went on forever. When he finally got to his destination at 9:00 p.m., the square was deserted. Where were the sailors and prostitutes from Rechy's novel? David had a beer in an empty bar before tackling the thirty kilometers back to his motel, this time feeling his aching calf muscles. The next day, a motel employee exclaimed: "Downtown L.A.? No one goes there! It's dangerous at night!" In short, he had ultimately understood what he had been told in New York when he had decided to come out here: "You don't drive? You won't be able to do anything in Los Angeles, David. Go to San Francisco instead!"

What happened the following two days was to become part of his personal mythology. At the DMV, where he had been driven in the morning by his only contact in Los Angeles, a sculptor with whom his New York gallerist had put him in contact, David had filled out a few forms with questions so simple that they seemed to be addressed to a five-year-old child. Thus he had inadvertently taken, and passed, the writing portion of the test. "Come back this afternoon for the driving test," they told him, although he had never driven a car in his life. The sculptor had helped him practice for a few hours in his pickup truck, which had an automatic transmission. It was easy. Despite a few mistakes, David had obtained his driver's license that afternoon. The next morning he bought a used Ford Falcon. All of that happened in two days—on his fourth day in L.A. It was incredible, and exactly what he had imagined life in Los Angeles would be. While he was driving his new car through the huge city, he saw a highway rising up in the air like a ruin in a painting by Piranesi, and he said with exaltation: "Los Angeles could have a Piranesi, so here I am!" A week later he was in a one-room apartment in Venice that he also used as a studio, and he was starting to paint with acrylics, which in the States were of excellent quality and dried much quicker than oil paint. He was getting to know local artists during openings at art galleries, which were all on the same street. He was introduced to Nick Wilder, a young Stanford graduate who would become his first California gallerist, to Christopher Isherwood, a English novelist whose books he adored, and he was going to bars where men would meet.

Reality rarely turns out to be what one imagined. In '63, when David had arrived in Alexandria during the Egypt trip paid for by the *Sunday Times*, he had discovered a boring provincial town instead of the marvelous bohemian, cosmopolitan city the poems of Cavafy had created in his mind. But Los Angeles lived up to his dreams: he had immediately fallen in love with that megalopolis that combined American energy and Mediterranean heat. Everything was a marvel: the eight-lane highways, the immensity of the space, the light, the ocean, the vast beaches, the brilliant colors of the vegetation under the sun, the white villas with flat roofs, the glass buildings, the geometric lines, the houses of the stars built in artificial styles, the blending of modernity and nature. And the ease of life there: no social classes, no labels, no traditions, complications, elitism. Everyone was equal and free, the bars were open until two in the morning—the perfect time if you wanted to work the next day. Pleasure without guilt, a blue sky, heat, and the ocean. And pools glimmering under the sun. He had seen them from the plane when he was landing the first time, a myriad of light blue patches that dotted the ground. A pool here wasn't a sign of opulence; it was just a basin you would dive into to cool off—and an excellent place to pick up men.

For the past two and a half years he had lived off and on between the United States and England. He liked that double life between the old world and the new. After a year in Los Angeles, he had gone back to London to prepare some exhibitions. Then he had spent the summer of '65 in Boulder, the fall of '65 in L.A., the winter and spring of '66 in London (with a stay in Beirut, where he had sought inspiration for a series of etchings illustrating a new translation of Cavafy's poems), and now he was going back to Los Angeles, where he would remain all summer and probably fall, depending on how he felt. On one side there was London and Bradford—his family, his oldest friends, and his first gallerist—on the other, Los Angeles—easy sex, drugs, rich collectors—and between the two, New York, where he stopped as soon as he could to see Henry and go to exhibitions.

In three years he had made only one mistake. The previous December, just before returning to London, he had encountered a boy in a bar in Venice. After spending a few days with him, he couldn't imagine being without him. "Why don't you come with me?" Bob had never been out of Los Angeles. They even had to delay their departure so he could get a passport. They drove across the United States with one of David's English friends, who kept telling him he was crazy. Bob hadn't liked New York: it was dark, noisy, and dirty; it reeked. "Europe is really different," David had said. "You'll see." But Bob hadn't been impressed by the trip on the *Queen Mary* in the deluxe cabins paid for by David, or by the royal welcome they had received from close friends at the Waterloo station, or by London. It was old. "Old": a fatal flaw. Bob only wanted to take drugs and fuck. One evening they had found themselves seated in a bar near Ringo Starr and David had told him who their famous neighbor was. Bob hadn't blinked: "Don't the Beatles live in London?" As if it were perfectly natural, since they lived in London, to run into the Beatles on a street corner—or to run into the queen, for that matter! David had been forced to admit that he had never met anyone so stupid, and even if he found him incredibly handsome, after a week he could no longer stand Princess Bob. He sent him back to Los Angeles on the first flight he could book, and swore he would never make that mistake again. What he had thought was love was only desire.

He was already in California and was approaching L.A. Night had fallen. He would arrive late that evening, but there would surely be someone who would open the door, and a mattress on the floor to share. Having given up his studio in Venice, David would spend the summer at his friend Nick's. Nick, who didn't care about his material surroundings, had barely furnished the small apartment he rented, but was very welcoming. As soon as David got up in the morning he would jump into the communal pool.

He was very excited when he walked into his class on Monday morning, filled with the enchanting visions that had accompanied him on his trip. But where were the blond, tanned surfers? The room was full of students in their thirties, even forties, wealthy housewives who must have been bored at home after their children had left the nest, or would-be teachers who looked nothing like the models in *Physique Pictorial*. They stared at David with curiosity. With his huge, black-framed glasses, his platinum blond hair, his tomato red suit, his mismatched socks, his tie with green and white polka dots, and his matching hat, he stood apart from the other instructors. David sighed at the thought of the coming months.

He was introducing himself to his students when the door opened. A young man walked in.

"Excuse me, is this class A200?" he asked hesitantly.

"It's the advanced painting class," David answered, since he didn't know the course number.

"Oh, sorry. I made a mistake."

Taking a few quick steps, David placed himself between the boy and the door.

"Why not give it a try? It's not difficult..."

The student looked at him timidly. He was very young, still a teenager. His eyes were light brown, with long lashes, he had wavy brown hair, velvety cheeks, sensual lips, and freckles on his nose.

"I'm from England," David said, "and, you'll see, I am a very good professor. I've even received the gold medal from the Royal College of London!" he added, with a self-deprecating smile.

This way of self-promotion wasn't very subtle, but he had noticed that medals impressed Americans. He wanted the student to stay.

"You've happened in here—have trust in fate!"

That last argument seemed to convince the young man.

An hour later, David was thrilled when he saw the drawing that the new student had done. He wasn't just perfectly lovely, he had talent.

"Your work is at the required level. You can stay, no problem."

"I haven't taken the prerequisites to enroll in an advanced painting course," the boy replied in his timid voice.

"Don't worry. I'll take care of it."

There was no way that an administrative obstacle would come between him and Peter.

Yes, his name was Peter, like the friend with whom David had been platonically in love at the Royal College. Peter was a common first name, of course, but he saw it as a sign—a gift from fate.

Peter came to the next class. He had enrolled. At the end of the morning, he was gathering his things without hurrying, as if he had guessed David's intentions. David didn't even wait for the last student to leave before asking, "Want to grab a coffee?"

It soon became natural for them to have lunch together after the daily summertime class, to go walking on the beach in Santa Monica, to swim in the pool at Nick's apartment complex at the end of the afternoon, and to order pizza or fried chicken at his place while taking part in lively discussions on contemporary art. Peter, feeling intimidated, just listened. He made the trip every day by bus from the Valley, where he lived with his parents and two brothers. He was eighteen, came from a close-knit Jewish family, and had grown up in a wealthy suburb. His father sold life insurance, and his mother took care of the three boys. He had enrolled at the University of California at Santa Cruz, but regretted his choice because it didn't offer any art courses—that's why he was taking classes at UCLA during the vacation.

What developed between them over the summer was more than mere friendship. It was complete trust, along with an almost paternal tenderness shown by the twenty-nine-year-old man for the eighteen-year-old and an unreserved admiration by the younger for the older, a mutual concern, a longing to be together all the time, sadness when the time came to part—they hadn't noticed the hours passing—and an increasingly irresistible desire to touch each other. The end of the summer was approaching. Peter would soon have to return to Santa Cruz for his second year. Santa Cruz was a six-hour drive from Los Angeles when there wasn't too much traffic, and almost eight hours on the bus. How would they manage it? The question was hanging between them even when they didn't bring it up.

For the Labor Day weekend Peter's parents were going to Santa Fe with his brothers, and he was allowed to stay home alone. He invited David over, and David was touched when he saw the house and Peter's room decorated with posters, his drawings, and photos of him when he was a little boy, blonder, gorgeous. They spent the day by the pool. David drew Peter from the back in his swim trunks, lying on a lounge chair. Who made the first move? Peter mentioned being upset at the thought of their coming separation, David went over to sit next to him, put his hand on his shoulder, warmed by the sun. Or perhaps Peter took his hand, put it on his face, kissed it. Which one said "I love you" first? Peter was a virgin, he was an innocent boy who knew even less than David had back in Bradford. David deflowered him, but Peter asked only for that, his entire body trembling with desire. The act of love was on both sides a complete gift, entirely sweet, performed in gratitude and joy.

Peter left. David promised to come see him every weekend. A six-hour drive is nothing when you're driving to your lover. In Santa Cruz he rented a room in the very appropriately named Dream Inn, which they didn't leave the entire weekend. When they weren't sleeping or making love, David drew Peter, his round shoulders, still childlike but also wide and muscled, the shoulders of a swimmer, his slender and almost feminine waist, his nose covered with freckles, his mouth with the swollen, incredibly sensual upper lip, even his teeth, his beautiful, straight, healthy American teeth brushed with Colgate morning and night, his hair sweeping his forehead, the sparse, almost red hair in his armpits that David couldn't stop smelling, his penis,

43

his soft, firm, and white buttocks. When they separated on Sunday evening it was a ripping apart. Peter wasn't doing anything specific in Santa Cruz. Why didn't he transfer to Los Angeles? It would cause some administrative difficulties, but David, who had become friends with a painting professor close to the dean of the arts, said he would arrange things. The day when Peter learned that his transfer to UCLA for the second semester had been approved, he leapt up and down in the motel room.

David thought of Aristophanes' concept of love, which he had once read in one of Plato's dialogues. He felt he had found his other half. Their bodies and their souls interlocked perfectly. Peter was intelligent, sensitive, delicate, he had a sense of humor, and was so gorgeous! And he loved David, his mind, his humor, his accent, which he found refined, his kindness, his way of drawing and painting, his energy, his face, his smile, his solid body of an English peasant, his muscular arms, his hands.

For the first time David was passionately in love with a man who loved him back, and for the first time he painted real life—not an idea, not something he had seen in a book. He painted Nick in his pool, and Peter getting out of Nick's pool. He painted the water. The movement of the water, its transparency, its shimmering, which he stylized with wavy lines, the splash rising up when a diver hits the water, the only trace of a body that has disappeared under the surface. How could you depict something that was pure movement and lasted only a fraction of an instant, like an orgasm? He used thin paintbrushes and spent fifteen days with the most absolute concentration painting all the little lines of the splash. Two weeks for something that lasted two seconds.

For Christmas he brought Peter to London. He was of course afraid because of the bad experience of the year before. But Peter had nothing in common with Bob. He loved London. He loved everything that was old; he delighted in rummaging through the antique shops on Portobello Road, not far from Powis Terrace, where David lived. He met David's friends, who thought he was charming. "David and Peter." Their names were associated more and more often. They were a couple.

Back in Los Angeles, given the lack of intimacy in Nick's apartment, they moved in together on Pico Boulevard, where David had rented a studio in the fall. Peter told his parents he was sharing a house with some other UCLA students. When his father discovered the truth, there were scenes, shouting, his mother crying, all of which he described to David, who laughed and sympathized with him. His parents demanded that he see a shrink. He agreed out of respect for them, even though he couldn't see how those sessions would make him "normal." Peter and David's pleasure at finally being able to live together was so intense that neither those family problems nor the lack of comfort in their apartment could undermine it. The very small apartment was in an old, run-down house in the heart of a poor neighborhood in L.A., and whenever they turned on the lights, cockroaches skittered away. But it was a paradise because it sheltered their love. Peter spent the days at the university and David painted at home. In the evening they went out, went to the movies, ate at the Mexican restaurant on the corner or at a Japanese restaurant where David discreetly passed a small cup of sake to Peter, had dinner at Nick's or at their friends Christopher and Don's house. Peter wasn't old enough to be served legally, and David no longer felt the need to go to bars. They drank California white wine, which was the only thing in their refrigerator.

While leafing through a magazine David saw a Macy's ad showing a bedroom, whose strong diagonal lines he liked: it looked like a sculpture. That's how the idea for a painting was born: from a composition that was suddenly formed by chance in his mind, when he didn't expect it, like an apparition that emerged out of reality or from an image. There was a bed in the foreground, covered with a bedspread with sharp angles. He decided to put Peter on it, lying on his stomach, in a T-shirt and socks, no underwear, and painted him from photos, being mindful of the shadows cast by the light entering the window. He first titled his painting *The Room, Encino*, but at Peter's request changed the title to *The Room, Tarzana*, the name of the neighboring town, since Peter's family lived in Encino and he was afraid that someone might recognize him. "Recognize your butt?" said David, laughing, because you couldn't make out Peter's features, and his buttocks were right in the center of the painting.

In the spring, David received a prestigious award in England acknowledging avant-garde painters, the John

Moores Prize from the Walker Art Gallery in Liverpool, for his painting *Peter Getting Out of Nick's Pool*, in which he had painted Peter upright in the pool, from the back, naked, with water up to the middle of his thighs. By distancing himself from abstract painting, by going against the current to do what he wanted, he had won his wager. It was as if the austere English critics wanted to celebrate his love for Peter and for California. He gave half of the money he won for the prize to his parents, so they could visit his brother who had moved to Australia, and with the rest he bought a used convertible Morris Minor, in which he took Peter and one of his friends from the Royal College to France and Italy that summer. Peter sat in the front next to him, Patrick squeezed his long legs into the back. Everything excited Peter, the steep, narrow roads, the landscapes, the Tuscan hills and cypresses, the villages, the Mediterranean, the museums, the wine, the food, the cheap antiques which he began eagerly to collect. His enthusiasm delighted David.

They visited Rome, spent a week on the beach in Viareggio, then drove to Carennac, a village in southwestern France where Kas, his gallerist, had rented a château on the banks of the Dordogne River. He put David and Peter in a magnificent room, filled with antique furniture and a huge bed. Patrick painted watercolors, Peter took photos with the sophisticated camera his airline stewardess aunt had brought back from Japan, and David drew. He couldn't have been happier. Everything important to him was here: love, sex, friendship, good wine, work. In September, Peter flew back to Los Angeles because he had to return to school, the dear boy, and David stayed in London to prepare an exhibition that would take place in January at Kasmin's gallery. He did a large painting of Patrick in his studio on Manchester Street, which he finished just in time for the opening on January 19. Refusing to take himself seriously, he had ironically titled the exhibition *A splash, a lawn, two rooms, two stains, some neat cushions and a table . . . painted*, a simple factual description of the paintings to be exhibited. The critics loved the pools, the modernity of his rigorously geometric shapes with straight lines, and the light suffusing his works: he had truly become the painter of California. The success pleased him, of course, but it hardly made up for the physical pain Peter's absence was causing him. So he left London as soon as he could for New York, where he met his lover, whom he had persuaded to cut classes. For the first time, they drove across the United States together. As soon as they were approaching Los Angeles after being on the road for five days, David could smell the salty air of the Pacific: he was home.

They moved into an apartment that was much nicer than the run-down studio on Pico Boulevard. On the top floor, it looked out onto the ocean, was near the house where Peter, in the fall, had rented a room that David now used as a studio, and was a five-minute walk from the charming Spanish-style house where his best friends, Christopher and Don, lived and entertained. When they stepped out onto their balcony in the morning, they were immersed in the mist rising from the ocean and they had the impression that they were on the deck of the *Queen Mary*, in the middle of the Atlantic. David was planning to paint a large portrait of Christopher and Don. It wasn't a fashionable genre. He would surely be called retrograde. But he felt like doing it, and that was his definition of freedom: to escape from established ideas, shatter the expectations of others, break his own habits and his way of thinking. He never forgot the excellent advice of Ron Kitaj, his friend from the Royal College whom he saw fairly often, since Ron was spending the semester at Berkeley and came to visit him in L.A.: "Paint what matters to you."

Christopher Isherwood, novelist and screenwriter, mattered a lot to him. He was his closest friend in Los Angeles, even though Christopher, born in 1904, was much older. Like David, he was from the north of England (but from a higher social class), and had chosen to live in California for the same reasons: he loved the sun and the beautiful boys, and couldn't stand the prejudices of his homeland. His partner, Don, a painter David's age, wasn't yet eighteen when Christopher had met him on a beach in Santa Monica in 1954. David was intrigued by their great age difference and fascinated by their love story. They were the first long-term gay couple he had met. He wished for only one thing: to grow old one day with Peter the way Christopher had with Don. He wouldn't be painting their portrait; rather, he would be painting his dream.

He spent weeks drawing their faces. They posed in David's studio, and every time he told them to relax and forget he was there, Christopher crossed his legs, putting his left foot on his right knee, and looked at Don, while Don looked at David: the pose created itself. After Don left for London, where he was planning to spend some time, David continued to paint Christopher and saw him every day. Christopher told him about his life—rather his lives, because he had had several. After dropping out of school in Cambridge, he had left England at the age of twenty, lived in Berlin under the Weimar Republic—where his passion for a German man had inspired his most famous novel, *Goodbye to Berlin*—emigrated to the United States in 1939 with his friend, the poet W. H. Auden, then became a Buddhist and a Quaker before meeting Don on a beach in Santa Monica and settling down in California.

David knew of no one more free. But he saw Christopher devastated the day Don told him he was delaying his return from London. Though he feared losing his young lover, who was having a fling with another man, he was able to say to David: "Don't be too possessive of your friends, David. Let them be free." While he sympathized, David couldn't relate. Peter and he had only one desire: to be together.

The portrait is intimate and monumental. In the foreground there is a coffee table on which David arranged a few objects, piled-up books, a bowl of apples and bananas that brings a single touch of warm colors to the painting that is primarily blue, and an ear of dried corn whose symbolic shape seems to be a wink. The huge window in the top part of the canvas gives a sense of space, and David painted the closed interior shutters that turquoise blue that is the color of pools, the ocean, and the California sky. From the time of the Royal College, before coming to California, David had done a small drawing representing a man running, and had put a blue spot at the top of the work, which he had then called *Man running toward a bit of blue*. In fact, blue, especially that intense, bright, deep blue, the blue of Vermeer, was a color toward which one wanted to run, as if toward the sea. The geometric lines of the table, the window, and the large, square, woven wicker armchairs where Christopher and Don are sitting contrast with the softness of the human figures, which ultimately occupy only a small part of the space. It is both a still life and a portrait, a classic and very contemporary painting which reveals Christopher's feelings for Don and the depth of their relationship.

Happiness was possible. David felt it every morning when he woke up next to his lover, when he sat down in front of his easel, smelling the odor of the eucalyptus after it had rained, filling his lungs with the scent of jasmine and the salty air of the Pacific, meeting Peter for dinner. Happiness, unlike what the Romantics asserted, was not incompatible with creation, which did not necessarily come out of loss, but also out of plenitude. His decision to come to Los Angeles five years earlier when he didn't drive, an absurd decision according to his New York friends, had been the best decision he had ever made.

Peter longed to return to Europe, with which he had fallen in love during their summer in England, France, and Italy. He said he had been born in the wrong place at the wrong time. On a whim, he decided to submit applications to the Royal College and the Slade, and asked David for a letter of recommendation. When he didn't get into the Royal College, David, who expected as much—the school accepted only five or six students a year—tried to console him. He even took responsibility for the outcome: given his notorious reputation, he told Peter, his recommendation must have worked against him. A few days later another letter arrived, this time from the Slade. Peter opened it, shrugging his shoulders, not expecting anything. His eyes opened wide—he had gotten in.

For the first time their desires clashed, and they discovered a will in each other that love couldn't bend. David had no desire to leave Los Angeles, and especially not to go back to England, that elitist, nonegalitarian, and nondemocratic land of myopic nannies, where you couldn't order a drink after 11 p.m., unless you paid an exorbitant price to belong to a club. Since they had found a place on this earth where they were happy, why tempt fate elsewhere? And what did a true artist learn in a school? Peter knew the basics of drawing, he had talent, he didn't need anything else. They argued for a long time, bitterly, each sticking to his position. Granted, said Peter, institutions didn't create artists, but they helped them in their career—and even in their private lives! Wasn't it thanks to the gold medal from the Royal College that they had met? And his degree, which David didn't care much about, hadn't it served as a calling card when he was starting out? Hadn't Kasmin discovered him at the Royal College? To study in London

at a renowned school like the Slade was a unique opportunity: would David deny it to the man he claimed to love?
They would be gone just while he was studying, three or
four years. And if they didn't like it, they would just have
to cross the ocean again to return to their paradise. *Please,
David, please.* He accompanied his arguments with a caressing and persuasive tenderness. David gave in.

His fears weren't realized. Their life in London hardly
differed from the one they led in California. They moved
into the little Powis Terrace apartment, from which Peter
could get to the Slade in twenty minutes on the Tube.
David worked at home and, at the end of the day, impa-
tiently awaited the return of his lover after his classes or
work in his studio. Peter was disappointed to learn that
foreign students didn't have the right to an individual
work space at the Slade, but David found him a room in
his friend Ann's place; Ann, who had recently separated
from her husband, and who was an artist too, as well as the
mother of an adorable two-year-old with the poetic name
Byron—born just after the summer when Peter and David
had met—needed to supplement her income. She lived on
Colville Square, five minutes from their place—it was actually her ex-husband, a former friend of David's at the Royal
College, who had attracted him to this neighborhood. It
couldn't have been more practical.

Granted, the sky was grayer, but the cultural life was
richer in London than in Los Angeles, and David still had
more friends there. They were invited everywhere. They
went to premieres of plays, films, and operas, to Ossie's

fashion shows with Celia and Mo. They went to Kasmin's openings and those at other galleries. They dined at Odin, the chic restaurant owned by one of their friends. On the weekends they would visit aristocrats or artists who had châteaux with flower gardens in the English countryside. Peter, bewitched by it all, never stopped taking photos. David saw his country through the eyes of the young American and learned to love it again. On Sundays they gave teas with little sandwiches and cakes that reminded him of his childhood, and which quickly became so popular that they didn't have enough cups for everyone. The harmony between them had never been greater. Peter thanked David almost every day for granting him access to this world that was so much more refined than his native California. He had blended into London life as if he had always lived there. He was handsome, young, fresh meat amidst older men. Opportunities weren't lacking, and friends were not always loyal. (Even Henry, in Los Angeles, had swooped down on Peter like a bird of prey one day when he had found him alone in the Pico Boulevard studio, at the very beginning of their relationship. David had really laughed when Peter, as shocked as a modest virgin, had told him about it.) But there was no risk: in London as in L.A., they had eyes only for each other.

Summer arrived. They returned to the Dordogne to Kas's place, then went to stay with a friend of David's, Tony Richardson, an English filmmaker who lived between London and Los Angeles, and who had just renovated a hamlet in the hills above Saint-Tropez to make it a vacation spot for his friends and family—and for others. Tony was so welcoming that you didn't even have to let him know you were coming: you arrived when you wanted, you occupied one of the bungalows, you lived communally, you spent wonderful days by the pool, on top of a flower-covered hill that looked out over the sea. David and Peter met their L.A. friends there; California had moved to Europe. When autumn arrived, they spent weekends in Paris and traveled around France, always staying in the best hotels. It was so easy to drive as far as the Channel on Friday night, put the car on a ferry, and wake up in northern France on Saturday morning. Continental Europe was at their doorstep, with all its diversity and beauty—David had to admit they didn't have that in California. They particularly liked the spa in Vichy and its palace of Proustian elegance, the Pavillon Sévigné. It was great to be there alone, just the two of them, to get massages and spend relaxed evenings and nights together.

Peter brought him good luck. Their second year in London was professionally intense for David: the Whitechapel Gallery, in eastern London, had planned a retrospective of his works. He was following in the footsteps of the greats: that is where Picasso's *Guernica* had been exhibited in 1938, an act of protest against the civil war in Spain, and where the first exhibition of Mark Rothko in England had taken place in '61, when David was still a student at the Royal College, as well as the *New Generation* exhibition in '64. The retrospective would show all his work of the past ten years, his drawings, his engravings, the California paintings, the large portraits. He painted another double portrait, of Henry and his boyfriend, whom he went to draw and photograph in New York. That was when he experienced the limitations of the America he so admired: he fell ill, had a very high fever, and discovered to his stupefaction that, in this so very democratic and generous country, it was quite simply impossible to see a doctor if you didn't already have one. He was forced to wait for hours amongst the poorest of patients in a hospital emergency room.

Quite unlike the portrait of Christopher and Don, the new painting was predominately green and pink. Henry, his legs crossed, sitting in the middle of an art nouveau-style sofa made of pink velvet, in front of a window with a view of the Manhattan skyline, occupies the center of the canvas and faces the viewer. The light is reflected in his glasses. One of the polished shoes he's wearing appears under the transparent glass table, the other is on his knee. His boyfriend, standing on the side, in profile, wearing a beige raincoat, seems to be bringing a message or getting ready to go out. "He looks like the angel of the Annunciation," a friend told him, and David laughed because Henry had nothing in common with the Virgin Mary. The portrait isn't flattering, but a strength emanates from Henry, from his large stomach seen through the folds of his gray vest, his red tie, his slightly open mouth, his closed fist, the strip of skin visible between his sock and the bottom of his trousers, and again, it is a painting that evokes the relationship between the protagonists. But unlike that of Christopher and Don, the viewer senses that the relationship won't last. David immediately started another large-format painting, one that depicted Peter and Ossie from the back, sitting on iron chairs next to an empty chair (David's, who had gotten up to sketch the composition, and who was thus present through his very absence), in the lush green Parc des Sources in Vichy, between two rows of trees (the famous French landscaping style) that taper off into the distance.

On April 2, David was excited and nervous when he and Peter arrived at the Whitechapel Gallery opening. All of London was there. He saw again for the first time in ten years works from his youth that he had sold. When he was a student at the RCA he was still looking for himself, and his work was filled with references to French, Italian, American, old and contemporary, figurative or abstract painters, especially Dubuffet and Francis Bacon. But even at that time, he had absorbed their styles into his own, and his hand was recognizable, his forms, his theatricality, his taste for fun, his colors, his relationship with space, all of which was a precursor to his large double portraits.

His first retrospective at the age of thirty-two. He was on his way to becoming a well-known painter, even though he didn't like thinking about himself in those terms. His parents had heard him on the BBC and had seen photos of him in newspapers, people talked to them about their famous son, and the art gallery in Bradford had bought a few of his etchings. Requests for interviews increased, invitations rained down, people started to recognize him in the street. His works sold like hotcakes, especially the double portraits, luminous, modern, and instantly classic at the same time. Kas urged him to paint more, faster, because collectors were waiting. David didn't like working under pressure, but it was nice to feel wanted.

Compared to the exhilaration of his developing fame, his sweet domestic life with Peter sometimes seemed monotonous. They had been faithful to each other for almost four years. Desire was waning. Wasn't it written everywhere in literature—in Tristan and Isolde's tale, to start with, which he knew by heart thanks to Wagner's opera— that passion lasts three years? It now happened that Peter didn't want to make love, and he didn't even want David to kiss him. Peter accused his lover of not taking him seriously as an artist. David shrugged his shoulders. Peter was a twenty-two-year-old student at the Slade: he shouldn't exaggerate. After the retrospective, he complained of being only a sexual object in David's paintings—isn't that what all the newspapers were saying, and what their friends thought? David rolled his eyes and thought it best not to respond.

They argued the day before Easter when he was leaving to catch a train for Bradford, without Peter, since Easter, like Christmas, was strictly a family holiday.

"Are you ashamed of me?" Peter asked aggressively.

"Don't start."

"You're a real coward, David. I put up with my parents' anger for you."

"It's not about that, you know it. It's just not the right time."

They had already argued on that subject. David had explained that his parents, who had grown up in the provinces and went to the Methodist church every Sunday, knew nothing of homosexuality, except that the Lord had rained sulfur on Sodom and Gomorrah. He didn't want to shock his mother when she was almost seventy, and while she was worrying about her husband's ill health.

"It's never the right time!" shouted Peter, slamming the door.

When David returned from Bradford two days later with a chocolate egg, Peter was still brooding.

There wasn't much room in the apartment, which was also used as a studio. The adjoining apartment was for sale, and thanks to the success of his retrospective David was able to buy it. Work would begin in the autumn. Peter would supervise the workers and take care of decorating it. It was an activity he liked; he would feel useful. For a while, they talked only about their plans for the renovation. They had a common desire once again. Then in August, Peter left for Los Angeles to see his parents. When he returned at the beginning of September, he found David lovingly waiting for him. But their reunion wasn't what David had hoped for—they started arguing almost immediately. Peter was tense, irritable, and when David asked him what was wrong, he blamed his bad mood on jet lag, clearly a pretext. In the autumn, David took him to Northern and Eastern Europe, to the countries where the Whitechapel exhibition was traveling. The palaces of Karlsbad and Marienbad were wonderfully outdated, but Peter was upset because there were no antique shops; he held it against his lover, as if it were his fault. David, who could no longer talk to him without annoying him, found his moods tiresome.

Maybe Peter the Californian could no longer endure the long English winter, the sleet, the pollution, and he simply needed some sun. In February, David suggested they go to Morocco with their friend Celia, whom Peter liked a lot. The Hotel Mamounia was an oasis of beauty, of luxury, and of refinement, and the view of the gardens and palm trees from the balcony of their room where Peter was standing was splendid. David immediately saw the composition. When he took out his camera and his sketchbook, the young man, exasperated, threw up his arms: "Again!" He didn't want to pose. He wanted to leave the hotel, go to Marrakech, walk around the souk, visit the Gettys at their palace. "You're so young!" exclaimed David. "I'm done with all that." Peter accused him of being condescending and became so enraged that Celia, who came running over from the adjoining room, had a very hard time calming him down.

They agreed to spend the Easter vacation apart. They both needed some breathing room. A break. Peter would go to Paris and David to Los Angeles. There he found exactly what he had come for: a period of pure relaxation in the house of one of Nick's friends, a banker, where the party kept going full throttle day and night around the pool. Drugs were passed around, the boys were gorgeous, and the pleasure easy. After making love, he drew the men with whom he had just slept. He was feeling better, and he already missed Peter. In the airplane going back to London, he thought of him tenderly, impatient to see him and to make it up with him.

Peter was no longer available—he had met someone. David, who had just had his own fun, was hardly in a position to complain. And Peter was so young, he was only twenty-three. David had been his first lover; he needed to experiment. David had to let him live his adventure. He remembered what Christopher Isherwood had told him. The wise Christopher had managed to control his pain, Don had ultimately returned from London, and today they were happier than ever. David would find the strength to follow Christopher's lead.

Luckily, he had a lifesaver—his work. He had begun another double portrait, of Ossie and Celia, who had just gotten married because Celia was pregnant. It would be their wedding present. Ossie is sitting on a modern chair in a nonchalant pose, his cat on his lap, while Celia is standing next to the open window in a long, dark dress, her hand on her waist thickened by her pregnancy, next to a bouquet of white lilies. The phone on the right is white, too, as is the balustrade of the balcony and the cat, and all that white infuses the painting with a softness, reflecting that of Celia. David wasn't able to paint Ossie's feet and hid them in the plush of the rug. He also had trouble with Ossie's head. He kept doing it over without being satisfied, probably because he wasn't satisfied with Ossie himself, who was taking more and more drugs, becoming increasingly unstable, and was treating Celia badly. David had scarcely finished the painting when he accepted a commission, something he rarely did, for a portrait of the director of Covent Garden, who was retiring. It was better to stay busy. He was also thinking a great deal about another project, the idea for which had come to him when he had seen two photos lying side by side on the floor of his studio. One was of a boy swimming in a pool, the other of a young man in profile looking straight ahead. It looked like he was watching the swimmer. The composition, again born by chance, had pleased him, and he had immediately known what he wanted to paint: Peter in the position of the standing boy. Peter who for once wouldn't be the man swimming under the water, the object of the gaze, but the dressed man on the edge of the pool, the observer, the subject of the gaze, that is, the artist.

David begged him to come with him to France in July. If they returned to Carennac, the memory of the happy times spent in the château with Kas, his wife, and their guests, the river that reflected the pale yellow stone of the walls, the dinners in excellent company under the walnut trees, the exquisite grand cru Bordeaux, the mildness of summer evenings, would dispel their problems and resuscitate their love. Peter agreed to come, but wasn't very nice. He always seemed annoyed with David, even in public, in a humiliating way. He didn't want to pose or to make love. After a week he insisted they go to Cadaqués, where a friend had invited them. David gave in. When they arrived in the town in northeastern Spain after driving for a long time on winding roads in the heat, a horrible surprise awaited him: Peter's lover was there.

In three days Peter would leave for Greece, where he was planning to meet his parents, and David needed to spend some time alone with him. He begged him to skip a picnic on a boat with the group the next day. Peter couldn't see why he should deprive himself of a fun outing for a tête-à-tête with David, who would probably only criticize him. The day of the picnic, David followed him as far as the dock where all the guests had already gathered, waiting for Peter in the boat, including Peter's lover, a handsome Dane his age, tall and blond. David watched him jump onto the boat.

"Peter, if you go, it's over."

Peter didn't turn around. David's blood boiled.

"Fuck off!"

He had shouted so loudly that everyone turned around to look at him. He ran off. He packed his bag and left right away, traveling through the Pyrenees, stopping in Perpignan for the night, then driving to Carennac as quickly as the winding roads of the Dordogne allowed.

When he got out of the car in the courtyard of the château de Carennac and saw his friends, Kas and his wife, Jane, Ossie, Celia, and Patrick, he burst into tears. He already regretted getting angry. He tried to reach Peter on the phone, but had no luck. They couldn't separate for a month with those words "Fuck off!" ringing in their ears. He had to return to Cadaqués. He and Ossie drove off in the stifling summer heat, traveling for two days and stopping only to sleep.

Peter didn't seem happy to see him.

"What are you doing here? Go away."

"I can't leave now, Peter. I've been driving for four days, I'm too tired."

Tears were rolling down his cheeks in spite of himself. How could Peter be so cruel? Their friends intervened, and Peter softened a bit. The day before he left for Greece, they managed to talk, without shouting, without insulting each other. David felt better when they parted.

He had an entire month to reflect on what had happened. He was going to change. He would become less self-centered. He had taken Peter for granted. From now on he would listen to him, would pay more attention to him, think about complimenting him on his paintings and photos, would tell him what an essential place he had in his life. David remembered his own youth. He, too, at twenty-three, had felt lost. It couldn't be easy to live with an older artist who was already successful. He would show Peter that he respected him as a being distinct from himself, with his own life and his own will. He had been egocentric. Absorbed by his work, he had allowed distance to grow between them. But there had been extenuating circumstances. The retrospective wasn't an exhibition like any other; it represented ten years of his work.

When Peter returned to London in September, he told David that he needed more time. He put a mattress in his studio. At least he was still living down the street, with their friend Ann. The renovation that had caused such disturbance and noise the year before was done. The now huge apartment decorated with designer furniture that Peter had chosen was magnificent, and the spacious bathroom covered in bright blue tiles had a circular shower with multiple jets, which David dreamed of trying out with him. He had to be patient, allow him time and space. He painted a still life in which the objects scattered on a glass coffee table exuded a solitude that reflected his own. And another, of a red rubber lifesaver in a pool, a mirror of his melancholy. The days went by, in sadness, each one the same as the one before. He couldn't sleep without Valium. Some nights only the thought of his mother prevented him from swallowing the whole bottle. A friend, seeing how depressed he was, took him to Japan. David had wanted to go there for a long time, but Tokyo seemed ugly and polluted, the beauty of Kyoto didn't move him, and he couldn't stop thinking of Peter. He ended up calling him one evening from the hotel, only to hear, from thousands of miles away, these words that broke his heart: "It's over." In all of Japan he liked only one painting, entitled *Osaka in the Rain*, which he saw in an exhibition of traditional-style Japanese painters.

When he got back to London he threw himself into his work. The only person he could tolerate was his mother. She didn't know the reason for his sadness, but he sensed that she would have liked to carry his burden for him. She called him "my dear boy," was always ready to pose for him without ever complaining of fatigue, respected his work, and was overcome with gratitude when he offered her a bouquet of tulips, a dress, or a television. Deep down, he was waiting for Peter to return. It was just a matter of weeks, or of months, he was sure of it. Peter would ultimately exhaust the pleasures of novelty and end up realizing that their love was unique. There was a task to accomplish beforehand, like a trial in a fairy tale. He would create the painting that would give Peter back his dignity by representing him as an artist, and not as a lover.

The work resisted him. David spent hours examining it without understanding what was wrong. He tried to repaint the figure, to rework the swimmer and the surface of the water, but the problem persisted. One morning, when his gaze went back and forth from the photos to the painting, concentrating intensely, he had a revelation. The angle of the pool was wrong. Consequently, the entire painting was wrong. It had to be redone. "You're crazy!" Kas exclaimed. The canvas on which David had already spent six months appeared perfect to him. In any case, David didn't have time to start again before the exhibition that opened three weeks later, on May 13, at the André Emmerich Gallery in New York, his first solo exhibition since 1969. According to Kasmin, the problem existed only in David's mind; he couldn't let go because he couldn't let go of Peter. "No," he replied, and promised that the painting would be ready.

He worked like crazy. He brought Mo, his model and assistant who had become a close friend, to Tony's vacation spot above Saint-Tropez, where he had often gone with Peter. The latter had had the nerve to stop there at the end of the summer on his way back from Spain with his Nordic lover, but Tony had refused to let them stay, for which David was grateful. In spite of the coolness of the water in the early spring, David made Mo swim for a long time in the pool while taking photo after photo of him, then made him pose on the pool's stone edge in Peter's pink jacket. Back in London, he worked nonstop, even at night, because a young filmmaker who was doing a film on him offered to loan him lamps that were as bright as daylight. In exchange, David had to put up with the presence of the stranger in his studio for an afternoon. For ten days he didn't sleep. The work was completed the day before the opening. With the paint scarcely dry, he rolled the canvas and sent it to New York.

It was his most beautiful painting, more beautiful than the portrait of Christopher and Don, more beautiful than *Le Parc des Sources, Vichy*. Haloed in the light that bathes his bright pink jacket, his face, and light brown hair, Peter watches the swimmer in the transparent water, looking like an angel, but an angel with a real body casting a strong shadow on the edge of the pool. In it one finds both the strong diagonals and the green perspective of *Le Parc des Sources, Vichy*, and the intense, attractive blue of the portrait of Christopher and Don. This painting reflected the strength of his love for Peter. It was a portrait of the sky, a portrait of the water, a portrait of love, a portrait of an artist. Peter wouldn't be able to see it without acknowledging David's love for him.

The painting was bought right away; Peter didn't come back.

Henry arrived from New York for the summer, and took David to Corsica. Henry was a friend with a sharp tongue and cruel humor, but on this occasion he showed an exquisite patience, ready to be bored to death by David, who had only one subject of conversation—rather, of a monologue. He didn't wonder *whether* Peter would return, but *when* he would return. It was the only question he asked. When would Peter realize that David was the love of his life? When would he be done with the necessary experimentation of youth? David conceived a new double portrait of two London friends, a dancer and a seller of old books, who had met through him, or rather thanks to Peter. Their age difference was the same as that between Peter and him. If he painted them, perhaps he would understand the secret to a stable relationship. "You'd do better to paint your parents," Henry suggested. "It will give you time to reflect on your relationship with them. It would be an excellent form of psychoanalysis." Henry was only half joking.

David could no longer stand to be in London, where each couple of men in the street seen from the back, one svelte with brown hair, the other tall and blond, made his heart skip. And when he ran into Peter—which necessarily happened since they frequented the same world, the same galleries, the same friends—he had to pretend that he was doing well and stop himself from staring at his lover whose body was forbidden him. It was intolerable. The art world disgusted him. He learned that the man who had bought *Portrait of an Artist* in New York, pretending to be a private collector, had resold it in Germany for three times what he had paid: that painting in which he had left his soul had become the object of a speculation. He now had to finish the double portrait of the dancer and the bookseller, which would be the centerpiece of his next exhibition. He looked at the unfinished canvas and could no longer see the point. He hated the Powis Terrace apartment. He had to leave. He was lucky, no doubt, because he had the means. But he would have preferred a miserable cabin at the ends of the earth with Peter over this luxurious life he now had. After the Christmas holidays, which, like every year, he spent in Bradford with his parents, his sister, and the only brother who still lived in England, he flew to Los Angeles and rented a house on the beach in Malibu, where Celia and her two boys, one and three years old, joined him.

Her heart had been broken, too. Ossie continued to cheat on her and treated her very badly. She had to put up with him, for her sons' sake. Celia, a close friend of Peter's, criticized his cruelty, and had taken David's side. David, a longtime friend and former lover of Ossie's, had taken Celia's side. Everything about her was soft, her face, her smile, her curls, her light eyes, her voice, her babies. She was so pretty. David couldn't stop drawing her. Every morning he drove the forty miles to his Hollywood studio, and every evening he drove back to the house on the beach where Celia and the boys were waiting for him. She had prepared dinner, they opened a bottle of wine, drank it looking out at the ocean after the children were in bed. Around 2 a.m., after talking for a long time—about everything, about Ossie, Peter, nothing—they lay on the same bed and fell asleep snuggling. Like a brother and sister. Or a bit more tenderly. David gradually had the impression that his body was thawing. Was it friendship or love? It was something sweet that protected them from solitude and sadness, a protection that was abruptly taken away when Ossie, after hearing about the new intimacy between his wife and his friend, arrived from London like a hurricane and whisked away his wife and children.

Without Celia and her babies, even the sound of the waves seemed grim to him. He went back to Europe. On April 8, when he heard on the radio that Picasso had died in Mougins, France, at the age of ninety-one, he burst into tears. It had been almost two years since Peter had left him, two years of which he had no memory: the emptiness seemed to have swallowed time. In contrast, he saw as if it were yesterday his arrival in Cadaqués and the hard, cold, loveless look that Peter had given him when he had gotten out of the car. "Go away." He now understood that he would never meet Picasso and that Peter would never come back to him. The world would forever be without Picasso and Peter. It was a world in which he didn't want to live.

He didn't kill himself. He received an invitation to participate in an homage to Picasso. The man who had been the master printmaker for the Spanish painter, Aldo Crommelynck, taught him a new technique that he had just perfected and that enabled him to create color etchings as quickly and spontaneously as in black and white. By teaching the English painter a method that he hadn't had time to teach Picasso before his death, he made David Picasso's heir in printmaking. For the first time in two years, David managed not to think of Peter. The pleasure that this new technique brought him, the long days spent collaborating with the printmaker, absorbed his negative energy.

Henry joined him again in the summer and they spent a month together in Italy, in a villa that David had rented in Lucca. They were supposed to write a book together on David's life and work—it was Henry's idea. David drew his friend while they chatted aimlessly, drank exquisite wine, listened to operas, and smoked enormous cigars by the pool. The book didn't get very far, but David didn't feel alone, and life was beginning to flow in his veins again. He even found the strength to play a trick on Henry one day when, his notebook on his lap, he saw Henry sitting a few meters away, posing. Henry, who was a bit vain, liked having his portrait done. For more than a half hour David alternately studied him, then leaned over his page, back and forth, with a concentrated look, while his friend hardly dared to move so as not to disturb the session. "Can I see?" he finally asked, and when David held up the drawing of Mickey Mouse he had spent the half hour fine-tuning, the surprise and anger mixed on Henry's face was so comical that he burst into joyful laughter.

Perhaps, after all, life was possible without the man one loved. Perhaps he would never again experience the passion he had felt for Peter, perhaps there would never again be a perfect union, but there remained the perfection of friendship, the beauty of the cypresses on the hills, and the joy of working. And if he forgot Peter, if he managed to live without him, mightn't he return? No one was attracted by sadness and melancholy, but by lightheartedness, strength, happiness. David swam in the pool an hour every day, got tan, his shoulders became muscular, and he took care of his body. He knew that Peter needed him. He had heard of his financial difficulties and couldn't help thinking of him when he read the terrible ending of *Madame Bovary*.

The day following his return to London he let Peter know through a common friend that he would be happy to see him and help him out. The response was that Peter didn't need or want to see him.

Alone in the big silent Powis Terrace apartment, he was stricken with depression. He realized that he had spent the summer deluding himself. Whereas he thought he was regaining his strength and finally distancing himself from Peter, he was only waiting for him. He had even managed to convince himself that Peter must have changed his mind during the summer and was going to run back to him!

They had loved each other for five years, had been separated for two. He was now thirty-six and Peter twenty-five. How could he, who had always been so happy, so full of energy, so meant for happiness, be destroyed by this obsessive thought that invaded him like a weed? And yet he had felt well in Lucca with Henry. Why in London did he feel the absence of any desire except to die? Love was an addiction.

How could he get Peter out of his blood and become himself again? Leave London once more? Move to New York to be close to Henry? Leave, yes, but for somewhere where he wouldn't risk running into Peter, where no one had known them together, far from friends whose patience in the past two years he had exhausted, and who would no longer put up with hearing the name Peter again.

He chose Paris, where Tony Richardson loaned him an apartment that he owned in the Sixth Arrondissement.

From the building located on a little street between the boulevard Saint-Germain and the Seine, right next to the Procope restaurant, everything was accessible by foot: the Louvre, where he went in the afternoons; the art and experimental movie theaters; the Seine, which was greener than the Thames; the Café de Flore, where he went to drink his morning coffee and eat a buttered *tartine* while reading the newspaper; La Coupole, where he met friends for dinner in the evening. The studio was an oasis of calm in this lively neighborhood full of students, artists, and intellectuals. Celia often came to visit him, and he drew her. He made new friends, including a French designer and his partner, and a couple of American artists who had been living for twenty years in a small railroad apartment where they also worked. The idea that the man, who worked in the room at the back, couldn't go out without his wife seeing him amused David, who decided to paint them in their apartment. He would still cry when he thought of Peter, but he rediscovered the pleasure of wandering around and observing the street scene instead of being lost in himself. He met a French student at the Beaux-Arts, Yves-Marie, who became his lover, and got close to a young Californian, Gregory, whom he had met in Los Angeles at Nick's apartment and who lived on the nearby rue du Dragon.

He had spent six months in Paris and was beginning to feel better when he went to London to see the work of the filmmaker who had lent him his powerful lamps two years earlier. The film was called *A Bigger Splash*, from the title of his best-known painting. The narrative thread was extremely vague. The camera followed people who were part of David's life: Mo, his assistant, who expresses his fear that David might go to live in New York; his friend Patrick, who stands in his studio, mirroring the portrait David had done of him; Celia with her first baby; Kas in his gallery during a fake telephone call asking David to paint more quickly because buyers are clamoring; and Peter, of course, having tea and chatting with Celia, strolling in the streets of London or diving into a pool. There were images of Powis Terrace, of the bathroom with the bright blue tiles, and even of New York, where, David now remembered, the filmmaker had accompanied him for an opening. None of it seemed of much interest, and he could have done without the images of Peter, which caused a painful clenching in him.

Then something dreadful appeared: Peter in bed with another man. David was horrified, but he couldn't take his eyes off the screen. For several minutes, each second of which stuck a very sharp needle into his skin, Peter and that man were caressing each other, kissing, taking each other's clothes off, while the camera focused on Peter's lips, cheeks, nose, freckles, rounded back and buttocks, bringing back all that David had suppressed deep down for years. The blow was so violent that the wall he had patiently constructed stone by stone for three years abruptly collapsed. Nothing was left but the pain of betrayal, a pain so raw that he felt he was naked and being stoned, one sharp rock after another. He felt betrayed not only by the filmmaker, but by Celia, by Mo, by all those who had participated in this charade. And by Peter, of course. Had his need for money led him to make this scene? If he was broke, why hadn't he asked David? Out of pride? Had Peter ever had any real feelings for him? Where was the boy whom he had loved so passionately?

At the end of the screening he could say only one thing to the filmmaker: "Please take out 'Starring David Hockney.' I am not a star. I am not a film star."

He would never again let someone into his life and steal images of his intimacy or bits of his heart.

He returned to Paris a wreck. For two weeks he couldn't get out of bed or see anyone.

Would the pain ever go away? Weren't three years enough?

But perhaps the tsunami caused by the film was the salutary crisis, like the spike in fever that leaves the sick person exhausted, depleted, in sheets soaked in sweat, while signaling the end of the illness. Or perhaps the shock of seeing Peter do such a vulgar and cruel thing enabled him to realize that ideal love was only a fantasy. Or perhaps sorrow, like passion, lasts only three years. One morning when he awoke, he no longer felt the sharp agony that had sapped him for three years even when he attempted to cover it up. His obsession had evaporated. He was finally free and at peace. He saw Gregory more and more often and understood that their mutual feelings went beyond friendship. A new story was being born, cautiously, timidly, and surrounded by guardrails.

When a director proposed that he paint the set for *A Rake's Progress*, the opera by Stravinsky that would be performed at the Glyndebourne Festival, David had the impression that a door was opening through which he could escape. He had never designed a set for an opera before, but he seized the opportunity. It wasn't just a distraction. The new work took him far from the double portrait that he had decided to drop. He would move into a new phase: instead of experiencing things dramatically, he would enter the world of drama. *A Rake's Progress*, that story of perdition that had brought him success ten years earlier, would save him by giving him something other than himself to focus on.

The day of the premiere, a year later, his restaurant owner friend organized a picnic on the lawn of Glyndebourne, where 120 bottles of champagne were uncorked for David's thirty guests. The dishes were delicious and so abundant that he invited the singers and musicians. That extravagant party cost him more than what he had earned designing the set and costumes, but he had no regrets. There wasn't an ounce of sadness in that extraordinary bacchanal. He had climbed up from the bottom of the abyss and was now standing on the edge of life. Literally. While sitting on the grass, quite tipsy, contemplating the sun that was slowly setting behind the Sussex hills, he felt only love and gratitude for a world that offered such a beautiful sight.

THREE

THE CHILD WITHIN

Holding on to David's arm, his mother walked through the Hayward Gallery looking around at the abstract, dark, minimalist paintings. A thick rope placed on the ground caught her attention, probably because she could identify it. She stopped and read the name of the artist: Barry Flanagan.

"Did he make the rope?" she asked naively.

In the little group which, besides his parents, included his friend Henry, his assistant, and Gregory, his new partner, no one laughed. David explained to his mother, as informatively as he could, that it was conceptual art. Laura nodded her head like a good student.

"I prefer what you do," she said, sounding relieved when they entered the room where her son's works were hanging.

Their bright colors and figurative subjects contrasted with the works in the preceding rooms. His father stood in front of the painting of him and his wife and nodded his head, looking satisfied.

"That's really me, always busy. You can thank me, David. If I hadn't been hard on you this painting wouldn't exist!"

Henry chuckled, David rolled his eyes.

"Ken, you were quite right to shake your lazy son!"

"It is lovely," said Laura, "but I also liked the first version, with your reflection in the mirror. The only thing I regret," she added, "is that I'm not doing something, too. I would seem more interesting."

"Laura, you're fantastic. The queen mother," Henry said, affectionately putting his arm around the shoulders of the old lady, tiny and birdlike next to him.

"Thank you, dear. But where did you get that dress?" she continued, turning to her son. "I don't have one like that!"

"That blue looks really good on you, Mum, doesn't it?"

My Parents: it was difficult to believe that the work existed. No other painting had given him more trouble, not even *Portrait of an Artist*. Henry was right, as usual, when he had told him that painting his parents would be like psychoanalysis. After a year and a half of relentless work, David had given up: the more he worked on his father's face the more he looked like a mummy. "It's the effect of all that hasn't been said between you," Henry had told him. Perhaps, but it couldn't be now, when the old man was completely deaf, that they would start talking. He had called his mother to tell her of his failure. "My poor dear," she had said with her usual kindness, sensing his frustration. An hour later the phone had rung. It was his father, furious:

"What, you're giving up? After all that time you made us pose in Bradford, London, and Paris, even when we were tired or ill? You dare do that to your mother, the woman who fed you, who raised you, who has always been there for you? Don't you know what it means to her to be painted by you next to me? She was so proud!" He shouted as if his son was a naughty eight-year-old who had just done something really bad. David had had trouble containing himself. In a dark mood after he hung up, he had gone out to have a drink. At thirty-nine years old, it was time to take things in hand and solve his oedipal issues. But the next morning, he called his mother: "Mum, could you come to London? I'm starting over."

In the new version he got rid of the artificial triangle he had drawn between the figures, as well as the reflection of himself in the mirror placed on the table. All of that had distracted the viewer from the true subject, his parents. And above all he allowed his agitated father to pose the way he wanted. He painted him bending over a thick exhibition catalog that Ken had spontaneously opened on his lap as soon as he sat in David's studio, absorbed in his reading, his heels sticking up, almost moving, and his father suddenly came to life. His mother, sitting facing the viewer in the same pose as in the first version, her arthritic hands on her lap, has a softer expression, no longer crosses her feet, and wears a dress of that bright blue that David liked a lot, that blue toward which one wants to run. The painting, luminous, emits a sense of melancholy that fortunately his parents didn't seem to notice. The two old people are chained together, but separated, each enclosed in his or her solitude. When he completed his work, David realized that they presented a model he didn't want to adopt: to grow old as a couple, while still being alone.

It would be the last of his double portraits painted in a realist vein. The two other canvases hanging in the room, which his parents were now contemplating, and whose genesis Henry and Gregory were explaining, were very different. *Self-portrait with Blue Guitar* shows David drawing a blue guitar. That painting is incorporated into the one next to it: *Model with Unfinished Self Portrait*, where in the foreground a man (Gregory) in a blue robe is sleeping on a bed. These works also had their history. The summer before, when he had just started the new version of the portrait of his parents, David had accompanied Henry to Fire Island, two hours from New York City, which had a large gay community. One afternoon, while they were sitting on lounge chairs wearing white linen three-piece suits that contrasted with the nudity of the beautiful boys diving into the pool in front of them, Henry had read to him a poem by Wallace Stevens inspired by a Picasso painting. The poem was very long, made up of thirty-three stanzas that, when read in Henry's deep voice, mesmerized David and transported him very far from the island of pleasure and the sound of diving boys. The first stanza had been particularly striking:

> They said, "You have a blue guitar,
> You do not play things as they are."

The man replied, "Things as they are
Are changed upon the blue guitar."

Other verses caught his attention:

I cannot bring a world quite round,
Although I patch it as I can.

Or:

The color like a thought that grows
Out of a mood . . .

And the end was very beautiful:

We shall forget by day, except

The moments when we choose to play
The imagined pine, the imagined jay.

While he was listening to Henry, David had the impression that he was being handed the key to himself. He understood exactly what Stevens meant—about Picasso or about any painter. The blue guitar symbolized the talent of the artist, who couldn't play "things as they are" because they didn't exist in reality, only in representation. The blue guitar was exactly what his parents didn't have, and its absence made their lives dull. David had received a blue guitar—the power to imagine and to "patch together" the world—when he was born. He should thank his parents, nature, life, God. His gift was infinitely priceless.

Model with Unfinished Self Portrait is highly symbolic. David appears in the painting, but not on the same plane as the figure sleeping on the bed; he is in the background, painted on a canvas. As an artist he is apart, separated from Gregory or his parents, in another space. He had understood that his life would not be the same as that of most people. He wouldn't have a stable romantic life, because he was married to his art. Unlike Peter, Gregory was fine with David being entirely absorbed by his work; for his part, David was fine with Gregory having flings. They had an open relationship, which simplified everything. There was no frustration, no jealousy, no crises. Their arrangement had brought David so much peace that he could even see Peter again, and he paid him for doing little jobs. His former lover had posed for him when Gregory had to go on a trip. The feet of the person sleeping are Peter's. David saw them now without emotion; time had done its work. Granted, he wouldn't have minded making love to Peter again, but Peter didn't want to, and David resigned himself. At forty he had accepted what he was and what he wasn't, what life gave him and what it didn't.

Life was more than generous. He enjoyed extraordinary freedom. He had left Paris, where he was becoming too well known, and moved back to London. He had sold the apartment where he had lived with Peter—Ossie, then Mo and a group of druggies had lived in it while he was gone, and had left it in terrible condition—and bought another apartment on the top floor of the same building. The year before, he had spent a month at the Chateau Marmont in Los Angeles and rediscovered the pleasure of living in California. He was getting ready to spend the entire autumn in New York. He went on vacation on Fire Island, in France and Italy, and he traveled even farther, to Tahiti, on the way to Australia, where two of his brothers lived, to New Zealand, and to India with Kasmin—he hadn't liked that trip; he was shocked by the caste system and the terrible inequality between rich and poor...He would soon return to Egypt. Almost every year he had solo or group exhibitions in London, New York, Los Angeles, Paris, Berlin, or in other countries. He took a plane the way you take a taxi.

But above all, he had friends. A close-knit community on two continents, true friends whom he'd known for years or even decades, friends he adored who visited him every day or traveled with him. He used his fame to defend the gay community, particularly in London. He had fought against the customs bureau, which had confiscated his copies of *Physique Pictorial* and other similar magazines when he was returning from Los Angeles, under the pretext that they were pornographic. (He was very proud that he had put up a fight. By calling every day, by having discussions with increasingly important employees, discussions worthy of *Ubu Roi*, and by threatening to sue them, he had recovered his magazines and had won against Her Majesty's customs office!) More recently he had allowed a gay magazine to publish nude photos of him, and he had spoken up publicly in defense of a gay bookstore threatened by the police.

And he was having a lot of fun. It would have been hard to have had more fun. Vacations on Fire Island were fantastic. The party began with tea at 5 p.m. and lasted all night. Sex, poppers, cocaine, and Quaaludes... People went crazy, completely liberated, the poor mixed with millionaires, all equal when they were dancing, partying, doing crazy things—not exactly equal, since the true aristocracy was one of beauty. All that beauty on view was a real joy for a voyeur like him. In New York he would accompany his friend Joe McDonald, a model who knew everyone, to Studio 54, to the Ramrod, or to the gay baths, and his greatest pleasure was watching Joe, the most gorgeous man he had ever seen, pick up men right in front of him, as if theater and reality were intimately blended. Life had truly reserved a front-row seat for him. He wouldn't have changed places with anyone else in the world.

He felt so good that month of July 1977 when he turned forty that he dared to be himself all the way. After having taken a position as a gay man, he claimed his status as a figurative artist. The year before, there had been a huge controversy that had pitted the London art milieu against the general public, when the Tate acquired a work by the artist Carl Andre, 120 bricks forming a long rectangle and titled *Equivalent VIII*. Articles were written, accusing the museum of having wasted taxpayers' money in paying thousands of pounds sterling for that pile of bricks. In its defense, the museum's director had cited the example of cubism, which hadn't been understood and was ripped to shreds in its time. On the occasion of the annual exhibition at the Hayward Gallery, the Scottish journalist Fyfe Robertson devoted one of the episodes of *Robbie*, a popular TV program aired on the BBC, to contemporary art in England, and invited David to be a guest on the show. Fyfe Robertson detested minimalist and abstract art, which in his opinion was thumbing its nose at its audience. Playing on the homophony with the word "fart," he had even created the term "phart," for "phony art." Going into the room where David's paintings were exhibited, he had had the impression of living again: it was an oasis of light, of life, and of humanity.

Far from expressing solidarity with his colleagues who were being attacked by the journalist, David acknowledged that the Hayward Gallery exhibited a number of very boring works. He even dared to say on TV that it seemed to him that a painting should have a subject, represent something. He shared his mother's reaction in front of Flanagan's rope, and added that in his eyes, the question she'd asked raised a real issue. The making of art, handicraft, scorned by the London art critics who spoke only of ideas and theory and who formed a little incestuous circle amongst themselves, was part of a work of art and deserved to be acknowledged. In his opinion, there shouldn't be such a separation between the elite and the people. Why was it just abstract works, accessible only to a small number, that were considered "serious" art? Shouldn't art speak to everyone? Interviewed by Peter Fuller for *Art Monthly*, he reiterated the same ideas, adding that the Tate's collection was truly insignificant.

He wasn't afraid to say what he thought and to throw a bomb into the critics' circle. Art belonged to artists, not to theoreticians. After all, he had always moved against the current. And he had nothing against scandal, which drew attention to his work. But he was happy to leave London in the autumn and take refuge in New York, where he was able to paint in peace. In October a solo exhibition opened at the André Emmerich Gallery, where the same works that were exhibited in London were shown—to which was added the painting depicting Henry looking at reproductions hanging on a screen, which he had finished in the meantime. The evening of the opening, a crowd filled the gallery on Fifty-seventh Street. Emmerich was happy, because Hilton Kramer had deigned to come. Surrounded by a court that listened to him religiously, the great American critic chatted amiably with the artist. Kramer's name circulated reverentially from mouth to mouth. He was a god in his field, and his presence had the value of a consecration. It was clear that David, at just forty years old, could no longer be ignored.

A few days later, Emmerich called him early in the morning.

"Kramer's review has just come out. David, I'm sorry: he's made a mockery of us."

David was shocked. He didn't expect that. During the opening, the critic had seemed to like his work.

"Is it that bad?"

"It's harsh. Backstabbing. I don't know what bug bit him. He must have something against the English, or against your success. Luckily, your reputation doesn't depend on him. The reviews in the other papers are excellent, and everything has been sold."

"I've been painting for twenty-five years, André. Kramer isn't going to tell me what I'm worth. Anyway, in my opinion he's a has-been. His attack flatters me."

As soon as he hung up David ran out to buy the *New York Times* at the deli down the street. He read the review as he walked back to the apartment he was renting, not far from where Henry lived. Kramer began with some apparent compliments: the works exhibited in the gallery, he wrote, were pleasant, entertaining, and the public really liked them. "Why, then," he continued, "do I find them—well, superficial and even reactionary?" He believed Hockney's art was "a kind of 19th-century salon art refurbished from the stockroom of modernism." He spoke of the triumphant return of what could be called "bourgeois art compounded out of the very materials that once challenged and offended bourgeois taste." He concluded by saying that David was too much of a lightweight to do justice to Wallace Stevens's imagination.

David laughed. Kramer had wanted to massacre him. The article, with its rhetorical questions, was perverse. An assassination. It was always the same old argument—the serious versus pleasure—clothed in well-turned phrases. He cut out the review and stuck it on the wall of his studio—a little reminder of the stupidity of critics and of the abyss that separated them from creators. Of course they snubbed the notion of pleasure. Prematurely embittered, without any other talent than that of denigrating, they hated success, except that which they had artificially created with their pompous words!

Henry called him a bit later. He had just seen the review. He was sorry about it and wanted to know how his friend was doing. His sincere solicitude annoyed David because it revealed the power of the critic. He understood that he should expect curious, falsely commiserating, secretly triumphant, looks from people, and that he now risked being labeled. Ill will was universal and success attracted envy. He reassured Henry. Kramer hadn't hurt him at all.

"He calls works I spent years thinking about, as you know better than anyone, superficial! Total crap. But ultimately not surprising. It's a very small world, and I'm the one who took the first shot, after all. Kramer has surely read the article in *Art Monthly*. He's defending his clique."

He had more important things to deal with. Where should he live? Which city should he and Gregory settle in so he could get back to work?

That's the question he asked himself in the spring when he returned from Egypt, where he had taken his friend Joe McDonald and even Peter, without Gregory showing any jealousy. Life in London was good, but too busy. Too many friends stopping in, too many journalists wanting to interview him, too many people asking favors of him (a design for a book cover, a party invitation, a poster for a charity gala…). He felt drowned but couldn't say no. The publication of his autobiography in '76, the exhibition at the Hayward in the summer of '77, *The Magic Flute*, for which he had designed the set for the Glyndebourne Festival in '78, had made him too famous. He couldn't complain. But he missed his California years, when Peter and he lived in Santa Monica and he didn't know many people. He had done seventeen paintings in one year! How, at the age of forty-one, would he find such solitude again? In London it was impossible, and he hated his new apartment, with a view of the sky where the light was, granted, excellent, but where he felt isolated because he could no longer see the street scene.

The solution was obvious: Los Angeles. "You're just nostalgic for your Peter years," Henry told him on the phone. For once he didn't think Henry was right. When he was a child, he didn't have enough paper to draw on. Now that he had achieved fame, he lacked the emptiness from which painting was born. After designing the sets for two operas in a row and settling accounts with the past, he just needed a place to be alone and paint. In Los Angeles, he was still essentially anonymous, and the city was so huge and spread out that there was little chance he would run into many people. His instincts told him he should go there.

He was just going to spend a few days in New York (on his way to Los Angeles) to get his new driver's license—and to visit Henry and Joe McDonald—but his American printmaker, who had left California and moved to the suburbs of New York, insisted that David come and see the new technique he had just perfected. It consisted of printing color in paper pulp. The process was very messy, because you made the paper yourself and wallowed in water. In boots, wearing long rubber aprons, the two men cut out metal shapes similar to cookie cutters to use in printing the design right into the paper. David spent a whole day there, then returned the next day, and the day after, and decided to delay his departure. He worked with such concentration that he could stand for sixteen hours, scarcely stopping to eat a bite or to dive into the pool to cool off, because the August heat was torrid. The colors were extraordinary, amazingly strong and intense. He first did a series of sunflowers in homage to Van Gogh, the master of bright colors. He then wondered how to vary his subjects and thought of swimming pools. It would be an opportunity to use blue again. In the evening he took the train to New York, had dinner with Henry or went out with Joe, then, like Cinderella, returned home by midnight: he had to get up early the next day to go to Bedford. If he could have, he would have stopped sleeping. In a month and a half he did thirty paper pools. One morning, he was done. He had exhausted the fun of it. He flew off to L.A.

The heat there was dryer than in New York. He was happy to see again the wide streets bordered by low, white houses with impeccable lawns, the blue of the sky and the ocean, the air scented with jasmine and marijuana, the luxurious vegetation. His assistant had found him a small apartment on Miller Drive and a studio in West Hollywood, on Santa Monica Boulevard. He missed Gregory, who had gone off to Madrid with a boy he had met in Paris, but solitude was good, since it allowed him to think and to work without distractions. He finally had an idea for a large painting: he would paint the street scene in Los Angeles as experienced from a slow-moving car. It would depict the entire length of Santa Monica Boulevard, where his studio was, and every viewer would have the impression of sitting next to him in his convertible. Full of creative energy after his stay in New York, he got to work. Gregory returned from Madrid, tanned and handsome, his tenderness increased by his gratitude toward David for letting him have his fling. Their reunion was joyful; Gregory's eyes lit up when he saw the sketch of the new painting.

During the autumn, David, who spent two days a week in San Francisco teaching at the Art Institute, realized that he couldn't hear the voices of the female students, which were softer than those of the boys. He went to see a specialist, who confirmed what he feared: his hearing was deteriorating, he had already lost 25 percent. It was irreversible. "You can't hear girls anymore? What's the problem?" Henry joked. But the problem would only worsen. He would end up like his father, completely deaf. It was a very depressing thought. The doctor asked him if he preferred a hearing aid in the left ear or the right.

"If I wear two, I'll hear better?"

"Yes, but in general, people only wear one: it's more discreet."

For David only one thing mattered: to hear the music with which he lived at every moment in his studio and in his car. He ordered two hearing aids that Gregory proclaimed were very sexy after David painted one bright red and the other bright blue. There was no more reason to hide one's deafness than one's homosexuality. He had always had that positive attitude, and he would keep it.

For the time being, it was working in his favor. In February '79, there was an exhibition of his paper pools at the Warehouse Gallery in Covent Garden. The critics who had panned him the year before compared his new work to Monet's water lilies. Monet, no less! He had to be careful not to pay any more attention to their praise than to their attacks. The only thing that mattered was the pleasure he had had in creating that series. David was sure of one thing: pleasure, in work as in life, was the only compass. The same critics who had asserted that pleasure meant superficiality were now singing his praises. Their ironic turnaround—rather, their lack of consistency—was satisfying enough, but he wasn't painting for them: he wanted nothing more than to surprise himself.

He shared his success with his parents and his brother Paul, whom he brought to London and put up in the Savoy. For two days he devoted himself to his guests, treating them to the best restaurants and even taking them one evening to see a pantomime, as in the good old days in Bradford. There comes a time when one becomes the parent of one's own parents. His father, for once, didn't complain about anything, and his mother, for whom he bought a dress at Harrods, was as excited as a twenty-year-old. He was happy he could bring her such joy, his beloved mother whose daily life wasn't easy, living with a silent husband who was more stubborn than a child, who did not regularly follow his diabetes treatment and ended up at the hospital almost once a month to be put on an intravenous drip, indifferent to the concern he caused his wife. That was, moreover, what happened after their brief stay in London: again, Ken wasn't careful, and had to be hospitalized.

The phone rang at six in the morning, the day after David had returned to Los Angeles. When he picked up the phone and heard his brother's voice, he immediately guessed that it was bad news. His father had died during the night from a massive heart attack. He burst into tears. When his mother had told him that Ken had been hospitalized, he wasn't worried; they would give him an insulin infusion and he would get out of the hospital all perked up, as always. He hadn't imagined for a second that the old man, who in London a few days earlier had gone around everywhere and looked at everything around him with a curiosity that age hadn't diminished, would die. The conversation he had not had with his father would never happen. The word "never" took on new meaning. It didn't involve the past, but opened onto the future and encompassed eternity. David would never see his father again. Ken had disappeared from the surface of the earth, as intangible as if he had never existed.

David booked a seat on the next Concorde and flew to Europe. "You've come back to a sad house," his mother told him when he got to Bradford and took her in his arms, so small, frail, and alone that he felt closer to her than ever. He couldn't say a word during the funeral. Laura wouldn't forgive herself for not going to see her husband the day after he was hospitalized. A snowstorm had covered Bradford with a white carpet and the temperature had fallen well below freezing. Ken had told her to stay in the warm house, it wouldn't do any good for her to go out in that cold and risk getting sick, when he would be home in two days at most. He had been generous enough to think of her, her health, when he was lying far from his family on a hospital bed. She had let him die alone, in a strange place. She had given in to the temptation of comfort, and heaven had taken away her partner. She didn't express these thoughts, but David guessed them in the devastated look on her face. All he could do was draw her, as if in drawing he could extract the sadness from her heart with the tip of his pencil. He thought of the portrait he had painted of his parents, that image of solitude and silence. He had gotten it all wrong. Ken was perhaps not the most communicative man in the world, he was certainly self-centered and cranky, but he had always been there for his wife, and for fifty years she had never been alone. And David, that beloved son who thought he loved his mother and understood her better than anyone, would be gone in a week.

From Los Angeles he wrote to her: "I think you made a marvellous choice for a partner in life and I know in a way you are very proud of him. I know it must have been difficult at times but his motivations were like yours, always to kindness. I think the combination was wonderful. Keep cheerful." The words he wrote to soothe his mother's sorrow eased his own pain as well. They were true. David thought there was no reason for despair. Dead at seventy-five, Ken had had a long and very full life, he had been a good father and a good husband, he had fought for causes he was passionate about—against tobacco, against the war, against nuclear weapons—he was a man of convictions who had transmitted his tenacity to his children. He was still living through them and in their memory. He was dead, but his combative spirit was still there, that spirit that pushed David, passing through London after the services, to inquire about the Tate's acquisition policy, after learning that the museum—who had only two of his paintings, bought a long time before—had passed on the opportunity to acquire one of his paper pools at an excellent price. He gave an interview to the *Observer* and poured out the bitterness he felt after the death of his father. In the article, entitled "No Joy at the Tate," he accused the museum's director of favoring a soulless and purely theoretical current in contemporary British art, despite its mission to represent all movements.

It had been several weeks since the exhibition in London and his father's death, and his mind had traveled far from the large painting he was working on. He wanted to get back to it when he returned to Los Angeles, and walked into his studio, where the canvas was hanging on the wall in the back. It was Santa Monica Boulevard with its rectangular, low, and colorful buildings, its bright blue sky, its wide sidewalks, its palm trees and their shadows. There were a few figures: a black man in jeans, white tank top, and basketball shoes leaning against a door; a woman jogger with a cap on her head leaning against a post; someone walking; a person pulling a cart looking at the price of a car for sale.

The colors were those of California, sharp, contrasting. He had never seen such a boring painting. He recognized the frustration he had already experienced twice, while painting *Portrait of an Artist* and then *My Parents*, before the lightbulb moments that had enabled him to create his two best works. He had to be patient and have confidence. The feeling of failure was part of the creative process. Every artist—painter, musician, writer—knew this.

His mother's visit took his mind off his concerns. He had bought her a plane ticket so she could go see her two sons in Australia, one of whom had not been able to fly to England for their father's burial. She spent a month with them and, on the way back, stopped in Los Angeles for the first time. It was during the Easter holidays. David had also invited Ann, his London friend, with her son, Byron, thinking that the presence of this kind woman and her thirteen-year-old son would help cheer up his mother. Laura was in mourning, she seemed lost, absent at times, but she marveled at everything with her usual sweetness, and in particular at the constant sun and warmth. "With all this sunshine," she said one day, "it's wonderful drying weather, but nobody ever seems to hang their washing out." Her comment could make one smile in the land of washing machines and dryers, where most people were unaware that you could do your wash by hand and let it dry in the wind. David was surprised that he had never wondered about it, he who had spent his youth washing his own laundry—so he was already more jaded than he thought! He loved his mother's astonishment at noticing the absence of sheets flapping in the wind. That impressed her more than all the screenwriters, artists, and famous actors she met without being able to place them at Christopher and Don's weekly parties in their old Spanish-style house on Adelaide Drive—Dennis Hopper, Billy Wilder, Tony Richardson, Igor Stravinsky, George Cukor, Jack Nicholson, and others. David did delight her, however, by inviting Cary Grant, all of whose films she had seen, over for tea one day.

Her childlike innocence seemed to her son the most precious thing in the world. Only a child looked at the world that way, without being distracted by the stupid preoccupations of adults. Only a child observed ants that gathered crumbs, ladybugs, drops of water falling on leaves, puddles, and stones. David liked the company of Byron, who, an only son raised by a divorced mother, talked as well as an adult, but with the logic of a child. David had known him as a baby and had watched him grow up, since Ann lived nearby in Notting Hill, and he went to see them often when he was in London, but he had never lived with them for two full weeks. Byron, whose hair was as dark brown as his mother's was red, a nice-looking boy with large eyes who looked somewhat Italian, was interested in everything, asked a thousand questions, but also knew not to interrupt a conversation or a silence, and watched David paint without bothering him. He passionately wanted to win when they played cards. When he was with him, David felt both like a father and like a child.

Their stay, which he had anticipated with some trepidation, turned out to be wonderfully harmonious and lighthearted. They all got along so well, and California pleased his mother, Ann, and Byron so much that he invited them all to return as soon as they could. They would stay in more comfortable quarters, because he planned to move into a house, now that he was certain he would stay in Los Angeles, where he had found the perfect balance between solitude and community. During the summer Gregory found one in the Hollywood Hills. Located at the end of a cul-de-sac called Montcalm Avenue, hidden by vegetation, the property, not very luxurious but certainly spacious, was made up of several bungalows and had a pool. They moved into the house. It was decided that Laura, Ann, and Byron would come for Christmas.

David was working on a future show at the Metropolitan Opera, a triptych of French music from the first half of the twentieth century. It included a ballet by Satie, *Parade*—whose set had been designed by Picasso when the piece was created in 1917—*Les mamelles de Tirésias* by Poulenc, and *L'enfant et les sortilèges* by Ravel. The work as a whole would be called *Parade*. It was his third opera, and the first one in America. He had not yet found a solution for his large painting and needed a distraction. Designing a set was easier than painting; he just had to listen to the opera for hours and let his imagination take off. The music dictated the colors and shapes. The work was all the more agreeable since the New York director had had a model of the Met stage constructed for him, which even included miniaturized scaffolding, ropes, and lights.

This little theater delighted Byron when he returned to spend his Christmas vacation in Los Angeles with his mother and Laura. Everything enthralled the teenager: the new house hidden in dense vegetation that attracted raccoons, possums, and deer; the pool in the shape of a bean which he jumped into all day long, shouting with joy; the constant fine weather that allowed him to swim in December; and above all the extraordinary toy theater, thanks to which David was able to test his creations with exclusive performances for his little favored audience, during which he was seconded by his new fourteen-year-old assistant. Gregory, tired of rehearsing the show almost every day, was glad to be replaced. For Christmas, David, happy to finally have someone with whom he could share one of his greatest pleasures, took his guests to Disneyland. Byron and he went on all the rides and ended with David's favorite, Pirates of the Caribbean. When the boat shot into the darkness, and amidst the clanking of chains something brushed against their faces with a sinister sound, the child screamed and dug his fingers into David's arm; David was also shouting, out of joy, not terror, since he knew this ride by heart. Twenty minutes later, they met up with their English ladies—one with silver hair and the other with red—on the bench where they were waiting for them, and Byron hurried to his mother, yelling that she should have come, that it wasn't scary at all. David smiled. He didn't want a child, would hardly have had the time to raise one, but if he had had one, he would have wanted him to be like Byron: lively, curious, open, sensitive. A bit later, when they were headed to the park's exit at dusk, the two women arm in arm, David and Byron walking in front of them eating their cotton candy, Ann burst out laughing: "You're quite the pair, you two. I wonder who is the youngest!" David couldn't have been more flattered. At the end of the two weeks, which went by much too quickly, he promised Byron he would take him to the Grand Canyon next time he came. The boy's eyes lit up. He turned to his mother: "Can we come back at Easter?"

The adults laughed.

"Thank you, David. Now I'm going to hear the same question every day. Honey, let me point out that we have come twice this year and Los Angeles is not just around the corner! And you're spending the Easter holiday with your father."

"When you turn fifteen, Byron."

"That's too far away!"

David was sad to see them go.

On a trip back to England a few months later, he stopped in New York, where a large Picasso retrospective had just opened at MoMA. The Spanish painter's work filled the forty-eight rooms of the museum. Drawings, prints, etchings, paintings, sculptures, everything was there, and from all periods: blue, pink, cubist... The extent of the exhibition was stunning. It was as if Picasso had painted the entire contents of the Louvre, as if he had been at the same time Piero della Francesca, Vermeer, Rembrandt, Van Gogh, and Degas. A genius. A grand body of work, in every sense of the term. During the five days David spent in New York, he went to MoMA every day, particularly struck by a painting from 1951 that he hadn't known, *Massacre in Korea*, which Picasso had painted in the middle of the Korean War, inspired by Goya's *Tres de mayo* and Manet's *L'exécution de Maximilien*. Picasso's painting—which portrays a group of women and children with faces deformed by terror opposite masked soldiers that look like robots who are getting ready to gun them down—combined everything that mattered to David: perfect composition, reference to other works, a sense of time, humanity, and the importance of the subject.

He was almost forty-three. He was in the middle of his life. What had he done since his retrospective at the Whitechapel Gallery ten years earlier, in 1970? He had worked a lot, that was true. Lots of drawings and prints, sets for three operas, but how many paintings? Did he want to go down in history as a sketch artist or a theater designer?

The exhibition exuded too much positive energy for him to feel sad or worried. The pressing urge to paint swelled his veins. When he arrived in London for the summer, he quickly did sixteen paintings on the theme of music, inspired by his opera sets. He had but one desire: return to California, where he would be less distracted, and get back to his large work.

The day he returned, he received a phone call from the opera director informing him that a strike at the Metropolitan Opera would delay the performances of the triptych he had worked on with so much pleasure, and even threatened to cancel them. He was in a bad mood when he walked into his studio and saw *Santa Monica Boulevard*, hoping that the summer would have given him the distance necessary to understand what was wrong with it.

The painting seemed lifeless to him. A disaster.

In a corner of the room there was a little canvas that he had painted quickly, haphazardly, with no other goal than to try out new acrylic colors. That painting, which by chance resembled a canyon, seemed more alive and more interesting than the huge clunker on which he had been working for almost two years. To encourage him to paint more quickly, Henry had told him one day that there was no connection between the time one spent on a work and the result. Once again, his friend was right.

David abruptly turned to his assistant, pointed at *Santa Monica Boulevard*, and said, "Please take it out. Destroy it."

That night he couldn't sleep. He tossed and turned in his bed wondering how he could have spent a year and a half on a painting only to realize that it was a failure. He had entirely redone *Portrait of an Artist* and *My Parents*. But *Santa Monica Boulevard* was irredeemable, he was sure of it. Had he undertaken that work for the wrong reasons—just to do a great painting? Had his drive to paint left him at the same time Peter did? In healing from Peter, had he given up the desire that was at the origin of creation?

He had two hands, two legs, two eyes, an excellent technique, and yet nothing was under his control. Maybe he had lost his blue guitar. He was powerless to do anything about it. Maybe he would just design sets—for operas that would never be performed. He had to accept it. It was better than creating mediocre paintings.

He thought again of the Hilton Kramer review still tacked up on the wall of his studio and of what another great critic of American art, Clement Greenberg, had said eleven years earlier, when he went to the Emmerich Gallery for one of David's solo exhibitions: "This is no art for a serious gallery." He had always laughed at the scorn of the critics and at that notion of "serious." He suddenly wondered what they had seen in his work that he didn't. Didn't see, really? Hadn't Kramer's review struck his Achilles' heel, which was his fear of not being a good painter? David had always been aware of his weaknesses. He drew beautifully and was an excellent colorist, but there was something stiff in his paintings; he didn't have the freedom of a Picasso and never would. He wasn't able to create the form that went with his vision. Out of laziness or because it was easy, he fell back on the conventions of bourgeois naturalism, and it looked like he was just painting realistic portraits like those of a nineteenth-century artist. Kramer wasn't wrong. That was the entire problem with that new painting which, far from communicating the movement he had envisioned, remained flatly realistic—lifeless. Realism in painting wasn't the Real; it was a mere convention.

Wide awake, he was looking in the semidarkness at the ceiling of his bedroom when he remembered what Byron had said last Christmas as he was standing in front of the painting: "I like it, but it looks like a picture."

"A picture?"

"Yes. It doesn't look real. It's too...straight."

Ann had added: "I understand what he means. It's because of all those horizontal lines that are parallel to the edges of the painting." At the time, David had paid little attention to the remark, but it must have intrigued him enough to stay lodged in a corner of his memory. The teenager's words suddenly seemed luminous to him. Byron had identified the problem. David had composed his painting from photos he had taken on the boulevard. That was a mistake. The photos were limited by the fixed angle from which you were taking them, whereas eyes move around and change their focus when you look at something. And above all, you don't see only with your eyes, but also with your memory and moods.

He felt like a little light was blinking at the end of the tunnel through which he had been traveling ever since he had noted the failure of his project. Maybe there was still some hope, if he managed to change radically his way of painting. If he no longer composed from photos, but from his memory. If he no longer sought to create a great painting, but simply painted what mattered to him. He would be closer to the truth and to life.

His heart was light when we went into his studio the next day.

Since he had moved to the Hollywood Hills he drove twice a day between Montcalm Avenue and West Hollywood while listening to music, played on the excellent sound system he had had installed in his car. At the end of the day, after leaving the expressways of Santa Monica and Hollywood behind, he would climb the steep canyon roads bordered by luxurious and fragrant vegetation that reminded him of the south of France, and suddenly, after a turn in the road, he would see a brilliant ball of fire or the radiant blue of the ocean. He adjusted his speed in order to synchronize an aria of the opera he was listening to with the stunning view. It was not just a car trip; it was the most beautiful moment of his day. That is what he was going to paint.

He did a little trial piece that showed the route he took through the canyon. A winding road was depicted vertically in the middle of the canvas, surrounded by spots of vibrant colors that represented the hills and the vegetation with, here and there, trees or a house. This painting was completely unlike anything he had painted up to then—except the works he had done just to try out acrylic colors—and looked like a child's drawing. The second one was bigger, more ambitious: he painted the route from his house to his studio, in softer colors, with a technique that was somewhat pointillist. The undulating road went through the canvas horizontally, bordered by a more complex landscape that included hills, trees, low vegetation, but also a tennis court, a pool, an electrical pole, a grid map of downtown L.A., with the ocean on the horizon. Everything was on the same scale, as in maps drawn by children. These two paintings, and those that followed, were not traditional landscapes, but journeys through time, lively tales that charmed the eye with the balance of warm colors and geometric shapes. The critics would think he had regressed into childhood. But David had no doubt he was on the right path.

He hadn't wasted his time working on *Santa Monica Boulevard*, since he now knew why his old way of painting didn't work, or creating opera sets, because that work in three dimensions had changed his relationship with space.

The triptych was finally going to be performed, after a yearlong delay. In January 1981, in New York, where he was attending the final rehearsals for *Parade*, he met a cute, blond student at a dinner at Henry's, on Ninth Street, where David had recently moved with a young lover. He invited the student to come to the rehearsal at the Met that evening. When they left the opera at the end of the performance, the city was plunged in darkness: there was a blackout. The subway was closed, there weren't any buses, it was impossible to get a taxi. They had to walk from Lincoln Center to the West Village. David took out a Walkman, which impressed his new friend, because the gadget had just come on the market; he even had two sets of headphones. It was very cold, steam came out of their mouths when they breathed. The only light came from the moon and the headlights of cars as they walked down Broadway through Times Square and the Garment District, and passed the Flatiron Building; they were connected by the wires affixed in their ears, and by the music that exploded in them. The young man was handsome, he seemed sensitive and intelligent. Was a new love affair possible? Ian was twenty-two and David almost twice that. Ian lived in New York and David in Los Angeles. A generation and a continent separated them.

The premiere of *Parade* was a triumph. All the critics agreed that it was his *Parade*, that his set and costumes had transformed the triptych into a visual enchantment. When the director invited him to collaborate on a new show, David agreed, even though Henry had pointed out that it would be impossible to achieve the same success twice in a row, and that creating sets would again divert him from painting. That was true, but this work gave him a pretext to return to New York often.

Ian made himself available as soon as David called. They went to see exhibitions or films, and ate out in restaurants. David knew that Henry had met him in a gay bar and that the young man wasn't bashful, but he feared ruining their budding friendship with an unwelcome move. At the end of the year he suggested that Ian come to live in Los Angeles. He could study at the Otis School of Design, the equivalent of Parsons in New York, live at David's, and work for him. He would learn more in the studio than in classes. The idea appealed to Ian, who obtained his transfer and moved to L.A. in January 1982. It was the proof David needed. They soon shared his upstairs bedroom.

Life still gave you gifts at the age of forty-five. You just had to maintain a sense of fun and be daring: dare to shout out in pleasure or in fear, dare to say that you liked Disneyland, dare to eat cotton candy, dare to follow your desire of the moment, dare to destroy your work, dare to try something new, to play, to do everything adults don't allow. To stay connected with the child in you. He and Ian painted the house on Montcalm Avenue, which he had recently bought. They chose such striking colors that when you walked in you had the feeling you were entering a Matisse painting: bright red and green walls, a floor and balustrades of Prussian blue. They emptied the pool, and David painted little wavy, dark blue lines at the bottom.

Gregory didn't like the new arrangement, and David had to remind him that they had an open relationship, which Gregory couldn't deny since he had taken advantage of it. "But not at home, not under your nose!" his lover exclaimed. "It doesn't make any difference," David replied, somewhat dishonestly. But he was sincere when he begged Gregory to accept a situation that in no way diminished the strength of their bond. He loved him, they worked together, they were both traveling on the same path, pointing to the same future, a future that was indeed assured them by the pact they had made, basing their relationship on a more solid foundation than carnal desire. Faithfulness was a bourgeois notion. He had suffered too much with Peter, from being abandoned, from solitude. To no longer be alone, you had to keep a partner beyond desire. What they had between them—friendship, mutual respect, aesthetic affinities, work, tenderness—was more important. Gregory let himself be convinced, but as night approached and he became morose, to improve his mood he often resorted to drinking, smoking pot, or doing stronger drugs.

Right after Ian arrived, a curator at the Centre Beaubourg in Paris came to ask David to participate in an exhibition on photography and art. Once there the curator bought a large quantity of Polaroid film to photograph the photos whose negatives David couldn't find. When he went away, he left behind a large number of those expensive cartridges. The next day, David gave in to the impulse to use them. He photographed details in different rooms of the house from various angles.

While he was gluing together the photos for *My House Montcalm Avenue Los Angeles Friday, February 26th 1982*, he felt a sort of tingling in his veins. He recognized the sensation: he had had the same feeling when he had introduced letters and numbers into his paintings at the Royal College or, more recently, when he had created his paper pools in New York. There was nothing more important than that sensation of pleasure in work, which absorbed him the way a game absorbs a child. He had to follow it, without yet knowing where it would lead him. His grouping of thirty Polaroid photos allowed the viewer to move around from room to room, through space and time, unlike a single photo, which would have fixed only one moment. So it wasn't really photography, strictly speaking, rather "photographic painting." Ten years earlier, he had been shocked by an exhibition at the Victoria and Albert Museum in London called '*From today painting is dead': The Beginnings of Photography*. He was taking his revenge by using the photographic medium against itself. He was subverting its use by reinjecting time spans and movement into it.

He made 150 collages in a week. Then he started photographing people and painting portraits at the same time, inspired directly by his photomontages, of Ian, Celia, and Gregory, portraits that looked like cubist paintings. His addiction only became stronger when he bought a small Pentax camera and was able to make collages without the white Polaroid print borders that interrupted the spatial flow of the images. He imposed only one rule on himself: he couldn't cut the photos. But he wasn't obliged to respect the straight edges of the page. A feverish excitement prevented him from sleeping. He woke up Ian or Gregory in the middle of the night so they could admire his new collage. On the phone with Henry he talked about nothing else and had trouble pretending he was interested in the professional concerns of his closest friend. Henry told him he had gone crazy, and renamed the house on Montcalm Avenue "Mount Hysterical." David admitted, laughing, that Christopher had compared him to a mad scientist. The floor of his studio was littered with thousands of photos. He couldn't stop. He had just finished a composition using 168 photos. The technology fed his exaltation: you could now develop photos in an hour! The only difficulty was in convincing the employee at the lab to also print shots that seemed to be duds.

Compared to the joy he felt in experimenting with this new, fun process, nothing was really important—except, perhaps, the letter he received from his mother in July for his forty-fifth birthday, in which that wonderful, beloved woman brought up for the first time, in a series of choppy and convoluted sentences, the subject of homosexuality, confessing that she didn't know anything about it, but a few years earlier had bought The Reverend Leonard Barnett's book on the subject, *Homosexuality: Time to Tell the Truth*, in the hope that she would be able to understand her son better. She expressed her fear that she hadn't been a good mother, wondered if parents were responsible for this "particular creation," and thanked her son for never having held it against her. She wished him all possible happiness. This naive letter contained so much love and generosity, came from such a beautiful soul, that David read it laughing and crying at the same time.

As for the rest...The Stravinsky opera at the Met wasn't well received, as Henry had predicted. That didn't prevent David from accepting another proposal from the Met, this time for a ballet. Gregory was drinking too much and was becoming aggressively jealous when he was drunk. It was a shame, but he would ultimately understand just how much he meant to David and would settle down. His friend Joe McDonald got such serious pneumonia that he had to be hospitalized. David went to visit him in New York, shocked to see how the illness had changed him. But he was being well taken care of, he would get better. Ian told him that he was going back to live on the East Coast to be closer to his father, who had just been diagnosed with cancer. David accepted the departure of his young lover philosophically—at least it would make Gregory happy.

Henry came to visit. David had just one desire: to show him his photomontages and share his excitement with him, but his friend was only half listening. He was getting ready to quit his job as commissioner of cultural affairs for New York City, a position to which he had been appointed by Mayor Koch five years earlier, an exhausting job that had made him ill. When he mentioned his fear that he wouldn't be able to afford his medical expenses, David realized he had come to borrow money. His best friend was hoping to take advantage of him! They got into an argument. Henry accused him of being a miser and an egocentric, and left sooner than planned. In the twenty years that they had known each other they had never had such a serious quarrel.

In August Ann and Byron returned to spend their holiday in California for the first time in more than two years. As promised, David took the teenager to see the Grand Canyon. Byron adored the desert. David snapped hundreds of photos. He wanted to create a collage that would give the viewer the impression that he was contemplating the landscape with eyes all around his head, enabling him to see everything at the same time, the dry grass at his feet, the orange and yellow of the rocks and their cracks, and the mountains on the horizon. While he was sitting with Byron on a cliff, looking out at the infiniteness of the sky and the rocks reddened by the setting sun, he thought about the letter he had recently received from Henry, in which his friend told him how disappointed he had been. He reminded David that he had supported him in his most difficult moments, when Peter left him, when his father died; and the one time Henry in turn needed an attentive ear and support, the person he thought was his friend hadn't listened. His single-minded passion for his work made him selfish and deaf. David told Byron about the quarrel, and the boy responded without hesitation: "You should say you're sorry."

"But he's the one who insulted me! He wasn't interested in me or my new work. He just came to get my money!"

"It's because he needs it, right? It can't have been easy for him to ask you. Can you imagine?"

David sensed that Byron had caused the scales to fall from his eyes. He understood that Henry had humiliated himself and that he, David, had rejected him. A boy not yet sixteen had spoken with the wisdom of a sage—or the clarity of childhood. He thanked him.

He sent Henry a letter of sincere apology and offered to help. He also wrote to Ian to say that his door would always be open and to ask his forgiveness for having been so absorbed in his photomontages. They were no doubt less instructive for a student than seeing a painting in progress.

He had adopted the right attitude. Henry reconciled with him. Ian, two months later, returned to California.

FOUR

DEATH IS OVERRATED

One evening in November, when he was having dinner with Gregory and Ian, the phone rang. The person on the other end, David Graves, had been David's assistant in London and his friend since he had met him seven years earlier at the premiere of *A Rake's Progress* in Glyndebourne. He was also the partner of Ann, whom Graves had met at some mutual friends' home. When Graves said, "David?" the softness of his voice conveyed something David recognized right away, something almost metallic that he had heard in his brother's voice one February morning three and a half years earlier, like an absence of resonance: the voice of tragedy. Byron. Byron, who had just turned sixteen, Byron whom just last summer David had taken to see the Hot Springs, the ghost town of Calico in the Mojave Desert, and the Grand Canyon, and who three months earlier was in this very house next to him, laughing, playing cards and Scrabble, telling jokes, helping him choose seventy-six photos for his photomontage, Byron, who had given him the best advice. His cries of joy and fear at Disneyland when he was fourteen still rang in David's ears. Dead. Byron had eaten hallucinogenic mushrooms—which weren't illegal in England—and had gone onto the subway tracks in London, where a train had crushed him.

David flew to England. He didn't know what to say to Ann. There weren't any words. If his mother had been the living image of sorrow at his father's death, Ann was but a silent cry. He took her in his arms, they clung to each other like two drowning people and sobbed. She had lost everything. He couldn't even begin to imagine what a woman who had carried a child in her womb, who had given birth to him, who had raised him—so well raised!—who loved him with all her heart, all her body, all her soul, and who hadn't been able to protect him from himself, must be feeling. There was nothing sadder than the burial at the Kensal Green cemetery the afternoon of November 11. All his friends from his time at the Royal College were there, including Byron's father, Michael. That sadness David expressed in the photomontage he did immediately afterward. It showed his mother in the rain in the ruins of the Bolton Abbey, wearing a long, dark-green raincoat with a hood, all the sorrow of the world on her wrinkled face. He invited Ann and Graves to come to Los Angeles—and to stay there, why not? There would be fewer reminders of Byron than in London; the heat, the sun, and the ocean might help Ann survive.

On the way back to California he stopped in New York to see Joe McDonald, who had gone home after a long stay in the hospital. His condition had scarcely improved and he stayed in bed; his mother was taking care of him. At thirty-seven, he looked eighty. His flesh had melted away, leaving his body emaciated and gaunt, his sunken face skeletal. Nothing was left of his beauty. It was now known that he didn't just have pneumonia, but what was being called "gay cancer," a sexually transmitted disease that attacked the immune system. There wasn't yet any treatment for it. David talked with Joe about his new work to distract him and, with his permission, took photos of him for a photomontage.

David's mother, Ann, and Graves spent the holidays in Los Angeles, as they had done three years earlier, during that Christmas that had followed the death of David's father. Now it was the oldest that took care of the younger. While he worked with Graves on the set for a ballet that the Metropolitan Opera had commissioned him to do, Ann walked with Laura and cried on her shoulder. Tony, their filmmaker compatriot who lived in L.A., invited them to spend New Year's Eve with him. He had two daughters, the younger of whom was Byron's age. Ann had to leave the party with Graves. In the evening, on the terrace of the Montcalm Avenue house painted in Prussian blue, they all played Scrabble, while David took their photos. He made a collage to which he gave the irregular shape of the words on the Scrabble board. On the right he superimposed a dozen images of his mother concentrating on the game (she excelled at it, won all the time), her serious profile, her arthritic hands knotted under her chin or moving the letters;

in the middle, eight photos of Ann, partly overlapping, and showing her reflecting with an absorbed air, her hand on her forehead, or laughing because she had finally found a word that would give her barely six points; on the left were photos of Graves, turning toward her tenderly, his face full of compassion, and smiling when she seemed happy; farther to the left the cat was playing on his side or was watching them, imperturbable. The harmony of the colors was astounding. The gray of his mother's dress and hair mirrored that of the game board; the red of Ann's hair was the same red as the painted table, and the blue of her dress and the yellow of her collar went with the blue, yellow, and red jacquard of Graves's sweater. Thanks to the photomontage, there would forever be the memory not of a fixed moment in time but of a chain of moments during which the Scrabble games had distracted Ann from her pain.

He continued his photomontages in England when he took his mother back home—he brought Ian over for the first time—then in Japan, where he had been invited to give a lecture. On that trip, Gregory went with him. While he was photographing the Ryoan-ji Temple Zen garden in Kyoto, he noticed that his new work technique enabled him to alter the perspective. A normal photo of the garden would have transformed it into a triangle, whereas the photomontage gave it back its rectangular shape, the one experienced by the meditative stroller as he walked around. After leaving Japan he stopped in New York to attend the final rehearsals for the ballet whose set he had created with Graves's help, and every day he visited Joe McDonald, who was once again in the hospital, so ill and weak that you had to put on a mask and gloves when you went into the room. It was the end. Ann joined him in New York to say goodbye to Joe, who had become a friend.

On April 17, Joe died. All of gay New York attended the funeral, the same crowd that filled the bars, the clubs, and the gay baths, which were now closed, and who danced all night long on Fire Island. People laughed when they remembered the hot moments with sexy Joe, and a moment later they became solemn and anxiously wondered who would be stricken with AIDS next. By one of those quirks of fate that life creates with indifference and that makes you think you're schizophrenic, Joe's burial took place the same day as the dress rehearsal for the ballet at the Metropolitan Opera. David went from one to the other. That afternoon he had given the eulogy for Joe that he had not had the strength to give for his father or Byron, and shuddered when he saw the casket being lowered into the grave; that evening, in a dark mood and with a sharp gaze, he verified that everything was perfect on the theater stage.

Like all his gay friends, every day he inspected his body and his back in the mirror, terrified that he would find a little black spot which would be the first sign of the plague. He hadn't been with as many men as Joe had, but he had had his share of flings and one-night stands—thank God, he had made the most of his freedom ten years before the epidemic appeared.

Joe, six months after Byron, four years after his father. The three ages of life stricken one after the other. Joe's death made no more sense than Byron's did. How could something as good, as healthy, and as liberating as sex cause death? And in the gay community, no less, which had fought tooth and nail to obtain its basic rights. How could that horrible illness strike them as if God had cast down another rain of sulfur on them?—something the abominable religious conservatives were quick to proclaim.

Shattered by sadness and fatigue, David needed a vacation. He took Ian, Graves, and Ann to Hawaii. Ann and Graves on a whim decided to get married after seeing an ad for a kitschy ceremony in a grotto, and David photographed them for a photomontage. When they got back, an exhibition of his new photographic works opened in New York. He was happy to read in *The New York Times* that he had "liberated photographic perspective from the tyranny of the lens." Yet the same exhibition in London in July was essentially ignored. No English critic could see the interest of his work with a camera. They thought the great draftsman was wasting his talent and his time.

He had recently had a studio built next to his house on Montcalm Avenue, on land where there had once been a tennis court, and he was eager to get back to painting. When the director of a museum in Minneapolis offered to organize an exhibition of his opera sets, David was going to turn him down: showing his drawings and sketches seemed boring to him. But then he thought of making paintings inspired by those sets, and of animating them with characters and animals. He threw himself completely into this new project. He had only a few months to create huge paintings and figures. He worked from dawn to nightfall with his assistants. Every day a new challenge consumed him. How could he represent figures in a way that wouldn't be boringly realistic? In a corner of his studio there was a pile of little empty canvases that he had never used. What if he assembled them—like his photos—painting on each of them a different part of a body: head, torso, legs? What about the animals? He wasn't going to go out and buy some stuffed animals in a toy shop! He cut them out of large pieces of thick polystyrene which he then painted. The work, very physical, had the added benefit of exhausting him: at night he collapsed and fell into a dreamless sleep.

While creating this fairy-tale universe through sheer hard work with the help of his assistants, he also drew and painted portraits—of himself, of Ian—inspired by the photomontages. In one of them he superimposed two versions of Ian, one showing his lover sleeping like an angel under the tender gaze of David, the other showing him sitting up, his hair disheveled, poking him in the eye, furious at having been woken up by caresses when he didn't want to make love. Ian burst out laughing when he saw the drawing: "Am I really as mean as that?" It was clear that he had come back to L.A. to have fun, not for David. David was no longer of an age to accompany the young man to the parties he attended every night, especially since he had never really been a party animal, even in the days when he followed Joe to the Ramrod or to Studio 54: his pleasure consisted above all in watching. Ian would get home at dawn, shortly before David got up.

At forty-six, he was feeling old for the first time. That's how he depicted himself in his drawings and paintings. He was no longer the eternally youthful blond boy with his mismatched socks and his striped polo shirt, but a naked man with an erect penis and a desire that he couldn't satisfy, or a tired man sliding slowly but surely toward an age that neither Joe nor Byron would ever reach. When Ian told him one evening that he was going to move out, David wasn't surprised. There was no scene. He had always known that Ian would leave him. It wasn't the end of the world, really, even if it hurt. He couldn't complain. He wasn't dead, and Ian wasn't either. He wasn't even alone, since Gregory was there, his loyal and faithful Gregory who worked, dined, smoked, drank, and talked with him late into the night. Gregory wasn't easy, drugs and alcohol could make him violent, and David had several times driven him to the hospital in the middle of the night, but he fought his demons. Sober, he was the best of friends, lovers, and assistants.

At the Walker Art Center in Minneapolis, where David had gone with Gregory for the opening of the exhibition of his opera sets, a book with a black cover titled *Principles of Chinese Painting*, by a Professor George Rowley, caught his eye in the museum shop. He had traveled to China a year earlier and was not very interested in Chinese painting, which seemed fairly uniform to him. He opened the book, however, without knowing why, and looked at the table of contents. A chapter called "Sequence and Moving Focus" piqued his curiosity. He bought the paperback and began reading it as soon as he got back to the hotel room.

It's an understatement to say he was enthralled by the book: it was earth-shattering. In its pages he found the theory behind everything he had been searching for during the past four or five years in his new photographic and pictorial experiments. He learned that, without knowing it, he had moved away from a limited Western tradition toward a more open Eastern tradition. European painting was forever linked to the invention of perspective in the fifteenth century. It was precisely the tyranny of perspective that David was trying to escape in his photomontages and his paintings that moved through space and time. Chinese artists did the same thing. In their work, they showed both interiors and exteriors and did not limit the gaze, which, in life, was not limited by perspective. "They practiced the principle of the moving focus, by which the eye could wander while the spectator also wandered in imagination through the landscape," David read. He could have written those words. Professor Rowley made a fascinating suggestion regarding one-point perspective: "Reverse perspective, in which the lines converge in the eye of the spectator instead of in the vanishing point, would have been much truer to psychological fact." The expression "reverse perspective" summed up what David had intuited years earlier when he had painted his *Kerby* from a work by Hogarth illustrating the gross errors that could arise when one ignored the laws of perspective: he believed at the time that those errors constituted a truer space than the so-called realistic space, because they opened the imaginary—what there was in us that was most individual and most subjective.

Should he believe in chance or fate? By what miracle had the director of the Walker Art Center in Minneapolis had the idea of organizing an exhibition that had brought David to this faraway city where he had found the book that summed up his work? It was incredible. A professor at Princeton had published this book forty years earlier, when David was six years old. The text he was reading gave his research the theoretical framework that every artist worthy of the name needs if he wants to be taken seriously. Even though he hated that notion of "serious," in the name of which the elitist and snobby art critics scorned his cheerful and colorful paintings, he had come to understand that his work was not determined by a mere hedonistic quest. It was an exploration, to quote Picasso, who had said something one day that David had never forgotten: "I'm not painting; I'm exploring."

Even though he was still haunted by the memory of the recent funerals of Joe and Byron, he had never felt so exhilarated. During the following months he met with curators of Asian art at the Metropolitan Museum and the British Museum. At the Met, in January, he was shown a seventy-two-foot-long scroll, a commission from the Chinese emperor dating from 1690. David spent four hours on his knees unrolling the parchment and observing each tiny detail, each little figure of A Day on the Grand Canal with the Chinese Emperor. He had trouble containing his excitement. This major discovery brought together his two passions—painting and music—because it had introduced him to another type of painting that, like music, had melodies and counterpoint, crescendos and diminuendos, and was experienced through time.

Back in Los Angeles, brimming with inspiration, he dove into a large painting that represented a visit to his friends Mo and Lisa's home, with a moving focus enabling the viewer to move through the rooms. He then painted a similar tour through Christopher and Don's place, from the studio where Don was painting the view of the ocean to Christopher's office, at the other end of the house, where Don's work, completed, was hanging on the wall. David simply made line drawings of the figures so they didn't distract from the true subject, which was the exploration, the traveling through time and space. The work was also an explosion of shapes and colors, with warm shades predominating over cool shades. These hues attracted and absorbed the eye before you even knew what you were seeing.

He was sorry he had to stop working to go with Gregory and Graves to the opening of an exhibition of his theater sets that was being held at the Tamayo Museum in Mexico City. On the way back, the car broke down and they had to spend five days waiting for it to be repaired in a small Mexican town, Acatlán, where there was absolutely nothing to do. Graves and Gregory drowned their boredom in tequila while David, ecstatic, contemplated the inner courtyard of the hotel thinking about his next painting: he would depict the stroll of a solitary walker around this courtyard in reverse perspective. There wouldn't be a figure, because the character inside the painting would be the viewer, whom

David would bring into the work through this new way of representing space.

He was becoming increasingly famous. Several exhibitions were devoted to him every year in different countries. Emmerich's sale of *A Visit with Mo and Lisa, Echo Park* had surpassed six figures, as they said in the States. His older brother, Paul, a former accountant who had been mayor of Bradford, had left politics and was now his business manager. Together they made a decision: David would no longer grant exclusive rights to a gallery and would control the fate of his work himself. He would be the master of his own house.

Because everything else escaped his control. Ian had moved in with a young actor, and even if it was a natural development, David had a bitter taste in his mouth that reminded him of Peter's betrayal. In Paris, his two closest friends had died of AIDS, one after the other. The month the second was buried, Christopher in turn died of cancer in Los Angeles. He had died at the "normal" age of eighty-two, after a long and full life, but his death left a hole in David that was as deep as the affection he felt for him. Close friends in Los Angeles, New York, London, and Paris had AIDS, with only a few months or a few years to live. Ann and Graves had decided to move back to England, even though David had begged them to change their minds: what would they do in gloomy London? Ann acknowledged that moving to Los Angeles had saved her life, and was infinitely grateful to David, but she now felt the need to return home and to get back to her roots. Despite several attempts, she had never obtained her driver's license, and life in L.A. without a car made her too dependent. Though he understood her reasons, he felt abandoned. A few lines in a letter she wrote to thank him after she left struck him: "In essence you're an island, David. Your mechanism is self-winding."

He didn't want to be an island. He liked having company, he wanted to have a family, friends, people around him, to help him not to think about all those who were dead or dying. But the last of them abandoned him, too. Gregory, returning from a month-long stint of rehab, announced one evening that he had to leave Montcalm Avenue if he wanted to stay sober.

"Unbelievable. Just don't touch the bottle, that's all."

"David, you drink every night, friends come over, drugs are passed around. It's impossible to resist."

"No. I'll help you."

"You're not listening to me. I've found an apartment in Echo Park, near Mo and Lisa. I'm moving out tomorrow."

"You're mad! What about me?"

"You only think about yourself! For me, it's a question of life and death."

"Don't you think you're being a bit dramatic? Is it the shrink I pay who put these ideas in your head?"

"This won't prevent us from working together."

"If you leave, don't ever step foot in here again."

The next day, Gregory packed his bags.

Gregory, who had shared his life for ten years, on whom he had always been able to depend and whom he had helped again and again, whose health care bills he had paid and whose insults he had endured without holding it against him, Gregory, whom he had always allowed to be free, was also betraying him, just when Ian had finally vacated the premises! David was so hurt that he had his brother send Gregory an official letter firing him like a mere employee, telling him to return the keys to the house, and even to reimburse David for the rehab clinic. Sorrow made him petty.

Only work saved him from the solitude in which his increasing deafness, the death of his friends, the departure of Ann and Graves, the break with Gregory, and his fear of a sexuality with fatal consequences had entrapped him. As soon as he was concentrating on a page, a canvas, or a screen, he no longer felt alone. The pleasure of discovering a new machine made him want to play with it while forgetting all the rest. He bought a computer on which he could draw with an electronic pencil. It felt like he was painting with light—an extraordinary experience. A new photocopying machine allowed him to enlarge and shrink the images, and even to photocopy real objects. You could create art with a humble office photocopying machine! Soon, he would be able to directly connect his camera to the printer and print out as many of his own lithographs as he wanted, as many times and as quickly as he wanted, on the Arches paper that he imported from France.

He was busier than ever. He had accepted a commission from French *Vogue*, which had given him carte blanche over forty pages—an excellent opportunity to expose his ideas on cubism and perspective, and to explain that there wasn't any distortion of the real when Picasso painted Dora Maar with three eyes and two noses, but that, on the contrary, the work showed an intimate reality: the face as it was seen by the artist who was getting closer to kiss her. *The Magic Flute* was going to be performed at the San Francisco Opera; he created sets for *Tristan and Isolde* for the new Los Angeles Opera; and he made the most complex of his photomontages for *Vanity Fair: Pearblossom Hwy., 11–18th April 1986, #1*, the crossing of two roads in the desert, in which even the road signs are made up of several photos, and in which the viewer can clearly see how altering the perspective renders the landscape more alive and more real. He feverishly prepared the second retrospective of his work that would open in two years at the Los Angeles County Museum of Art.

He did something else: he bought the house next to his and tried to convince Celia to move into it—but her teenage sons refused to live abroad, and she also had to take care of her aging mother. He ended up giving the house to Ian and his boyfriend, and they moved in during the summer of '87. It was better to purge himself of jealousy, bitterness, resentment, all negative feelings. Why not simply be friends? Wasn't Ian, that adorable boy, like a son? David had the incredible luck of having escaped AIDS. He didn't need sex anymore. Friendship was enough. For his fiftieth birthday in July, Ian gave him a little dachshund, the baby of his own dog. David had never had a pet before. His nomadic life on several continents made owning a pet impractical. He never imagined he would get attached to a dog. He couldn't believe what happened to him: he instantly fell in love with the puppy. He called him Stanley in memory of his father, who adored the actor Stan Laurel, and soon got a little companion for him so he wouldn't be lonely. He now had a good reason to stop traveling and to stay home with his dear dachshunds, close to his dear friends. For the New Year he and Ian threw a huge party in which several generations blended together. The house on Montcalm Avenue again vibrated with music, laughter, and noise, a celebration overshadowed only by the theft of his Picassoesque portrait of Celia, probably by one of Ian's young guests. The painting was never found.

The retrospective that opened at LACMA in April '88 showed thirty years of his work. The day of the opening, while he was walking through the rooms that contained drawings, etchings, portraits, the large California paintings, photomontages, opera sets, and even images from his own printer, David wondered whether his work didn't strive to be as ambitious as that of Proust, whom he had reread over the years. Proust's opus was built like a cathedral around a spiritual quest: the search for lost time—the search for the link between our different selves, which kept dying one after another. As for David, hadn't he, from the beginning, been searching for lost movement? He had always painted for the pleasure of it, following his impulses against all odds, without compromise, faithful to his own desires. This notion of pleasure, which critics put down and called superficial, didn't it rather contain something essential? Wasn't it the expression of life itself? Wasn't it the reason why he gave up a style as soon as he began to be bored with it, that is, as soon as life had drained out of it?

Hadn't he always needed to feel emotions in order to paint, and wasn't emotion (which etymologically came from the Latin word *motio*, movement) the same thing as movement, as life? His oeuvre was thus not just a personal refuge where he could escape pain; it was actually a construction that helped save painting, that art form which seemed to be doomed in the face of photography and film. David's work showed that painting was the most powerful art, the most real, because it contained memory, emotions, subjectivity, time: life. In that, it helped us overcome death.

For an exhibition in Arles, an homage to Van Gogh, David painted the artist's famous little chair from a reverse perspective: the "erroneous" perspective, just like the cubist paintings that revealed the reality of perception, gave the chair a dimension so human and affective that he immediately painted another one. He added it to the LACMA retrospective when it came to London in October after traveling to New York. People flocked to the Tate. The phone rang constantly. The public adored the exhibition. The art critics weren't absolutely negative, but called David "the lost child of contemporary painting" and found him as boring as an old school teacher in northern England when he talked endlessly about the tyranny of perspective. They didn't rave about him as they did about the new wunderkind of British art, Damien Hirst.

Their reticence awakened David's old provocateur spirit. A band of reactionaries in England thought they were guarding the entrances to "art" with their pitchforks? He would show them what a boy from Yorkshire who lived in Los Angeles was capable of. They were elitists? He would be egalitarian. Radically. He would make art accessible to all. He had already committed a subversive act the year before when ten thousand copies of an original "homemade" engraving of a ball bouncing had been distributed with the local Bradford newspaper. This time he would go farther.

He had been invited to participate in the São Paulo Biennial. He decided to send his works by fax. Henry, the commissioner of the exhibition, found the idea original; the biennial organizers thought it was a joke.

He wasn't joking.

The telephone lines weren't very reliable in Brazil; he had to send his work from his studio to another fax machine in Los Angeles, and then his assistant flew to São Paulo with the faxes in a suitcase. David didn't go. Since it was an exhibition by fax, he would respond to interviews by fax.

The fax machine was the telephone of the deaf. Ever since his sister Margaret, who was also hard of hearing, had made him buy one of the first machines available, every day he faxed drawings to his friends and family on two continents. They were often composed of several sheets of paper that had to be assembled when they arrived. First four sheets of paper, then eight, then twenty-four, and so on.

On November 10, 1989, the day after the fall of the Berlin Wall, he sent a fax of 144 pages, a stylized rendition of a tennis match, to the gallery that his young friend Jonathan Silver, his compatriot from Bradford who had become a rich businessman and an art patron, had opened in their hometown. It was in an old salt factory, and was dedicated to exhibiting David's engravings. He was alone with his assistant in his California studio, peaceful, in the morning light, introducing one by one into the machine the pages that would be received thousands of miles away, at the same moment, but in the evening, in a place where several hundred people were gathered to witness the assembling of the huge puzzle, applauding, laughing, and drinking wine. It was marvelous to think that this artistic performance had the power to erase distance while connecting day and night between continents: it was the best way to fight against solitude. It was his own way of tearing down walls.

Mo, his first model, his former lover, his friend, his assistant, had recently died at the age of forty-seven, after succumbing to the alcoholism that gripped him when his wife left him. Nick, his first friend and first gallerist in Los Angeles, died of AIDS in New York at the age of fifty-one, as did Kasmin's partner in London, one of David's close friends, too. Then he lost another friend who was only thirty-eight. The man had been working at Emmerich's gallery and, thanks to his contacts, had raised a million dollars to help those stricken with AIDS. The art world was decimated. When David took the plane now, it was to go to funerals. Churches, synagogues, and cemeteries were the places where he saw again those who were left. So many died that you couldn't cry anymore. Henry, who devoted his energy to helping AIDS victims, had been spared, thank God. But one evening Ian told him that he had tested positive. David took him in his arms and had to fight not to burst into tears.

"Testing positive isn't the same as having the illness. You're young, Ian. You'll survive. They'll find a vaccine."

You couldn't say or believe anything else.

In the midst of this hecatomb, a new man entered his life. David had met John, who was just barely twenty at the time, a few years earlier at a friend's place in London, and had invited him to California, where he had visited with his boyfriend the following year. The young man, a cook, had recently written to him asking for a job. He arrived in Los Angeles and David gradually fell under the charm of the twenty-three-year-old Englishman, tall and handsome, full of humor, sensual, who prepared the best fish and chips he'd ever eaten, and who loved all pleasures, food, cigarettes, drugs, alcohol, sex, swimming. John made him love his body again. He brought with him a vitality which David, at fifty-two, needed more than ever. He was no longer alone. A man was there with whom he talked, laughed, ate, made love. And what a man! When he saw the bronze torso of his lover, his muscular shoulders, his arms, his thighs worthy of the statues of Michelangelo, he couldn't believe his luck. It would certainly be the last adventure of that kind.

He had been living with John for a year when, one evening, he felt extremely tired. When he got up from the couch to go to bed, he collapsed on the stairs. John could hardly get him up, and he immediately drove him to the emergency room. A heart attack. If he had been alone, he would have died. The rapid response and the coronary angioplasty saved him.

When he left the hospital, the doctors recommended rest. He shouldn't work.

It seemed like a bad joke.

His friends had died of accidents, old age, alcoholism, cancer, AIDS. For him, it was work, his long-term constant ally against death, that had almost killed him.

Had killed him. One doesn't cheat death. He had lost the battle. Something in him surrendered. When he returned home after his surgery, he felt different, somewhat detached. He no longer felt the need to fight, to win, to convince the world of anything. Perhaps he had *wanted* too much.

Two years earlier he had bought an oceanfront cottage in Malibu, built in the 1930s, which Ian had discovered by chance, on a beach where dogs were allowed to run freely. It had belonged to a painter and included a studio, the smallest in which David had ever painted, but he felt good there. He installed a treadmill to do the exercises the doctors had recommended, he walked on the beach with his dogs every day, he changed his diet and ate healthy dishes that John prepared for him. John had suddenly assumed an almost paternal role toward his lover, who was much older than he. In the hospital, when he woke up after the operation, the first thing David had done was call Gregory, who had rushed to his bedside. They had reconciled, and Gregory began to work for him again. That was life: an ebb and flow. In his Malibu studio David painted little imaginary landscapes inspired by the movement of the ocean, which he watched from his window, and by the music of Strauss's *The Woman without a Shadow*, for which he was supposed to create the set with Gregory's help. For the first time he didn't give titles to his twenty-four paintings, but called them *Very New Paintings*, or *V.N. Paintings*. Were they abstract? What did it matter? The distinction between abstract art and figurative art existed only in the West.

While he was driving back from Chicago, where he had gone to attend the premiere of *Turandot* with John, his two dogs, and his two assistants, they stopped for the night in Monument Valley and slept in the RV. David woke up very early to photograph the sunrise. A storm had been forecast, and there were thick, black clouds on the horizon. When the sun appeared, it looked like gold on the rocky peaks. A bolt of lightning tore through the sky and a perfect rainbow appeared. David wouldn't have been surprised to see Moses speaking to the masses from atop the mountain. The extreme beauty of this sunrise erased the tension of the preceding days, when the RV had broken down in the desert and the constant barking of the dachshunds in the confined space had become unbearable for David's assistants. It made up for everything. The fights. Even death.

Tony Richardson, the friend with whom he had once spent wonderful summers in the south of France and family-like evenings in Los Angeles, died of AIDS in Paris, at the age of sixty-four. As for Henry, he called one evening, his voice strained. Ironically, it wasn't AIDS, but pancreatic cancer, like Christopher. It progressed very quickly, in a few months. David was there at the end, sitting next to his friend's bed, and drew him until the final moment. Henry was fifty-nine years old, only two years older than David, but he looked ninety. His fat cheeks had caved in, his face was gaunt. His mind, however, was just as alert as ever. And his vanity hadn't disappeared. "Draw me," he said to David, in a dying voice.

Henry had been his best friend since he had met him at Andy Warhol's in 1963, thirty-one years earlier. As soon as they arrived in a city together, they ran to the opera. Henry was the friend who knew every person and every event in David's life, who had participated in the creation of each work, to whom he spoke on the phone every day, and who had been there when his father, when Byron, when Joe, Christopher, and all the others had died; the friend who had always advised him and didn't hesitate to tell him what he thought, even harshly. In three decades they had had only one real fight, and after their reconciliation their friendship became stronger than ever. They had cried laughing together, in New York, London, Los Angeles, Corsica, Paris, Berlin, Lucca, Martha's Vineyard, Fire Island, Alaska...David had to chuckle when he thought of the day long ago when he had taken Henry, who was in London, to have dinner at the home of an old, deaf art collector whose mother, a close friend of Oscar Wilde, had taken in the Irish writer when he got out of prison in 1897. They rang the doorbell, the old lady opened the door, and Henry turned to David and asked in a trumpeting voice: "Let me get this straight: Oscar Wilde was her mother, right?" David was in stitches and unable to tell the old lady what he was laughing about. Without Henry, the world would be forever sadder.

He did small paintings of flowers and of the faces of his living friends. An exhibition entitled *Flowers, Faces and Spaces* (who still dared to paint and show flowers?) opened in London in a new gallery, since Kasmin, after the death of his partner, had closed his space. "Steep decline!" the art critics exclaimed.

The death toll kept climbing. Ossie was stabbed in his apartment by a former lover. Jonathan Silver, his compatriot from Bradford and close friend with whom he resumed the ritual of daily phone conversations following Henry's death, learned that he had pancreatic cancer and only a few months to live. The same illness that had killed Christopher and Henry, like a curse: Jonathan was only forty-eight.

The dark period had begun in '79 with his father. Then Byron in '82 and Joe in '83. After '86, it continued unabated. One, two, three, four friends every year. In Paris, London, New York, Los Angeles. No city, no continent was spared. Death everywhere, as in the Middle Ages during the Plague.

Maybe death was overrated.

Just before going to Mexico in '84, David had read a book that described the ritual practices of the Aztecs: Montezuma going into a temple and ripping out the hearts of five or six people before leaving, covered in blood, and resuming a conversation with the Spanish conquistador, the man he thought was a god, and who would destroy his civilization. The Spaniard, horrified by such a practice, thought the Aztec was a barbarian, as did any Westerner who read the book. But in the temple twenty-five thousand people stood in line for the honor of having their hearts ripped out. For those people, death didn't exist.

Perhaps death wasn't a tragedy, perhaps there was no reason to fear it. It was part of life. It was useless to fight it. One had to embrace it. And create works that would put joy in people's hearts. What the critics thought was of no importance. History retained the names of only a few rare artists: Rembrandt, Vermeer, Goya, Monet, Van Gogh, Picasso, Matisse. They had all offered an enchanting vision of the world. Art, like religion, shouldn't exclude anyone. It should be universal.

In Malibu, David painted. John, his young cook lover, had just left him following a fight. He was twenty-nine years younger than David: it was in the natural order of things. David wasn't alone, since he had his dogs, the most affectionate and most dependable of friends. The constant motion of the Pacific filled his windows. When he opened his kitchen door, the waves crashed at his feet. The ocean had come and gone that way for millions of years. His dachshunds watched the ocean, as he did. They weren't interested in television, where they probably only saw the flashing lights and flat shapes on the screen, whereas the regular beating of the waves hypnotized them. David painted the movement of the ocean. And he painted his dogs.

FIVE

HAWTHORNS IN BLOOM

What the hell was he doing here?

"To say that there weren't any great artists before optical devices is like saying there were no great lovers before Viagra!"

Susan Sontag spoke in such a booming voice that David had no trouble hearing her in spite of his handicap. The auditorium burst out laughing. Someone even whistled in the back; Larry held up the crutch that was leaning against his chair. His sciatica proved to be useful.

"Calm down, please! We're at a university symposium, not a circus!"

"Because David Hockney doesn't draw as well as the old masters," Sontag continued in a measured tone, "he concludes that they used optical devices. He has developed a theory from his personal experience. It is a very American process. He has truly become one of us!"

David smiled. When the famous American intellectual finished, the audience applauded for a long time. Larry then introduced Linda Nochlin, a professor with gray hair and the author of many important books. In the middle of her lecture, she stood up and took from a chair an article of clothing covered in dry-cleaning plastic, which she removed. The intrigued audience followed her movements. She hung on the wall a short white dress with a bold blue pattern of large, round-edged rectangles, which seemed to have come straight out of the 1960s.

"This is my wedding dress. I got married in '68."

The crowd of students, professors, art historians, journalists, artists, and socialites who had stood in line all morning on Cooper Square to get one of the four hundred coveted seats waited, delighted, ready to laugh.

"David," said Linda Nochlin, looking at him, "you say it's up to us to provide proof. Here it is."

With a dramatic gesture she pulled off the cloth that was covering a large painting also hanging on the wall: in it one saw, next to a man, a young woman wearing the wedding dress with blue rings, identical to the real dress and painted on the same scale. David immediately understood where she was going with this: she wanted to show that one could reproduce the motif of an article of clothing exactly without using an optical device. Which proved nothing.

"It's my wedding portrait by Philip Pearlstein. Philip?"

The American painter joined them on the stage.

"Philip, did you use an optical device or your own eyes?"

"My eyes."

Nochlin turned to David. "You see? Some artists are able to do it."

The audience applauded even more frenetically than they had for Susan Sontag. Someone shouted, "The old masters weren't cheaters, Hockney!"

Larry again had to brandish his crutch and threaten to kick the rabble-rouser out of the room.

David shook his head. He had never accused the old masters of cheating. The optical device was only a tool; it didn't create the painting. But three years earlier, at an exhibition of the drawings of Ingres in London, he had been fascinated by their extreme precision and the strength of the lines. He had bought the catalog and, back in L.A., enlarged the reproductions on his copy machine to examine them closely. One of the portraits had reminded him of the drawing of an eggbeater done by Warhol, for which Warhol had used a slide projector. David had then been certain that Ingres had also employed an optical instrument: the camera obscura, invented in 1807. After several years of research that had ended with a wall in his studio filled with reproductions of portraits, he had become convinced that European painters had been using optical instruments for centuries. He had even managed to date precisely the beginning of their use: in 1434, in a painting by Van Eyck, *The Arnolfini Portrait*. The lens didn't yet exist at that time, but a physics professor at the University of Tucson in Arizona, who was a specialist in optics, had come forward after reading an article about David's research and taught him that a concave mirror could have played the same role.

That research had enthralled him, because it revealed a continuity between the fifteenth and the twentieth century: the curved mirror and the lens were the ancestors of the camera. Up until cubism, the same perspective with a single viewing angle had ruled over European art. His theories, published in October in a book titled *Secret Knowledge: Rediscovering the Lost Techniques of the Old Masters*, had created a storm on the two continents. Nothing, proclaimed art historians, proved the presence of optical devices in the studios of the old masters. They accused David of wanting to belittle the great European painters. Only a few rare artists and scholars had come to his defense. The symposium had been organized to resolve the debate. The scale was clearly weighted on one side, and David had the impression he was attending his own trial. Most specialists attacked him like a college of cardinals trying to decide if they should condemn a heretic to the stake.

A trial, to be sure. What taboo had he broken for art historians to stand up as one against him? What were they afraid of? Their desire to keep art in an ideal world had something fascinating about it. David felt a bit like Robin Hood in his attempt to give art back to the people. In any case, it was reassuring to see that these questions evoked such passion in New York in December 2001, in an auditorium a thirty-minute walk from the site of the twin towers, three months after the event that had changed the world. But what was he doing being held hostage in this auditorium, when he had only one desire—to paint?

He had launched the polemic, to be sure. He now realized he didn't give a damn.

The next-to-last speaker got up. Rosalind Kraus, a professor at Columbia, editor of *October* and a diva of contemporary art criticism, reputed for her ferocity, projected on a screen the enlarged detail of Ingres's portrait and Warhol's drawing on which David's intuition was based. She showed that Warhol's lines, inert and of equal width—the result of technology—had nothing to do with those of Ingres, which swelled and shrank. An intelligent demonstration. The audience applauded for a long time.

Then it was David's turn. The grand finale. He walked up to the lectern. He was wearing a T-shirt on which I KNOW I'M RIGHT was printed in large characters. There was some chuckling, then the room was silent while he adjusted his glasses. You could have heard the proverbial pin drop. No one wanted to miss a word of what the famous painter was going to say in his defense after such a demonstration of his ignorance.

"I've learned many things," he began, speaking slowly while looking around at the audience above his glasses, "and I thank all the participants. These paintings are admirable. The truth is, we will never know how they were done."

He paused. Everyone was hanging on what he would say.

"Now I'm tired, and I want to go home and paint."

He walked off the stage in front of the dumbfounded audience: he had admitted he was beaten, okay, but this denouement lacked panache!

He hadn't admitted he was beaten. His conviction was not shaken. The earth revolves around the sun and not the other way around: that fact had ended up being proven without Galileo dying at the stake.

He really was exhausted. This business had taken three years of his life, three years during which he had painted only a series of portraits à la Ingres, using a camera obscura, in order to illustrate his theory. Three years earlier his mother had died, at the age of ninety-eight, surrounded by four of her five children. The autumn following her death, at the approach of the first Christmas—or almost the first—that he would spend without her in sixty-two years, David felt extremely depressed. Gregory had saved him from a dangerous addiction to alcohol and prescription drugs by sending him to rest at the FKK baths in Baden-Baden. When he got back from Germany he had dinner one evening with John, in London, where they were both passing through. At thirty-three, John had matured while staying the same—lively, funny, sensual, and warm—and a miracle that David would never have believed possible occurred: they fell back in love. John moved back in with him in Los Angeles, became his partner and his cook again.

A few months later, John had wondered whether David was sick. He was always tired and often fell asleep in the middle of dinner, at home or at his friends'. They had anxiously awaited the results of the medical tests: cancer, like Christopher, Henry, and Jonathan? No, just acute pancreatitis, a nonfatal illness, which from then on prevented him from drinking alcohol and caffeine. Then Stanley, his beloved dachshund, his first dog, had died at the age of fourteen. Then John and he, for months, had cared for one of their close friends in L.A. who was slowly dying of AIDS. David knew what had really motivated his optical device research: by awakening his old fighting spirit, it had given him the energy he needed to get through his mourning for his mother, for Stanley, and for his friend. Now it was time to get back to painting. He was sixty-four years old. Where was his great work?

Six years earlier, in 1995, the British prime minister, John Major, had borrowed one of his paintings from the Tate to hang in 10 Downing Street. An honor. But it was *My Parents*, painted in '75, as if David had done nothing as good as that in the following twenty years.

The older he got, the less he understood where inspiration came from.

The last time he had been truly inspired (and that completely by chance) was four years earlier, in '97, when he had spent the whole summer painting West Yorkshire for his friend Jonathan, who was dying and who had asked David, as a final favor, to do a painting celebrating their region of hills and farm fields, of modest beauty, which had been ignored by painters. David stayed with his old mother in Bridlington and almost every day visited his bedridden friend, who lived an hour and a half away. He traveled through the landscapes of his youth, the villages of Friday-thorpe and Sledmere, fields and farms where he had worked as a teenager—places to which he had emotional ties. Using bright colors and a naive style, he had applied his technique of altering focus to his Yorkshire pictures, which didn't simply depict landscapes, but his route from home to see Jonathan. Back in Los Angeles after Jonathan's death, he had continued to paint Yorkshire from memory before creating a huge painting of the Grand Canyon made up of sixty little canvases, a painting that measured over six feet by twenty-four feet, his largest format up to then. That had been his last period of intense creativity. Afterward, there were just the portraits done with the camera obscura.

After the New York symposium, he didn't want to stay in Los Angeles, where his friend had just died. In his state of indecisiveness, he decided to go back to London and agree to the request of Lucian Freud, who had been wanting to paint his portrait for several years. Freud needed some hundred hours of posing, and David had never found the time to do it. This would enable him to see the great artist's method and think about what would come next.

He spent two months observing. Freud's manner of painting, so different from his own, so slow, apparently as disorganized as his studio, was actually meticulous and profound. He also observed Holland Park, which he walked through twice a day between Pembroke Gardens and Freud's house on Kensington Church Street. From the end of March to the end of April he witnessed the birth of spring, which he had forgotten after several decades in California.

He went into the park by Ilchester Place and came out at Duchess of Bedford Walk. Every day he took the same route, and every day what he saw was different. He had never noticed so many varieties of trees, bushes, leaves, and flowers. Colors were perhaps brighter in California, but flatter, too. In England, the fog created a whole gamut of greens and infinitely diversified the palette. Some trees were already covered with white or pale pink flowers, like the cherry trees, the apple trees, and the magnolias. Others were hardly budding, and the myriad little leaves unfolding day by day formed a delicate lacy veil. In others, like the chestnut trees, the maples, and the beeches, an abundance of light green leaves weighed the branches down to the ground; finally, some, like the ash or the weeping willow with intertwined branches, took their time, like Lucian Freud, not in a hurry to leave winter. The lilacs, rosebushes, thyme bushes, sage, and bays scented the air.

David hadn't been expecting to enjoy himself so much when he was still recovering from 9/11, from the death of a friend, from the violence and the horror of the world. By eight in the morning, no matter the weather, the park was swelling with life. Schoolchildren in their uniforms ran and played with multicolored balls, dogs leapt freely, buds opened and trees became green, as living as the children and the dogs whose shouts and barking he didn't hear. One probably had to be deaf, and perceive one's surroundings only by seeing, to capture each detail with such acuity. He had never been so relaxed. How could a humble English park make him feel an exaltation greater than he had felt seeing the Grand Canyon or the desert? He was almost disappointed when Freud told him that the portrait was finished. An excellent portrait, by the way.

Was it that state of beatitude that led him to watercolors, that specialty of Sunday painters that he had always carefully avoided?

He was becoming senile.

It happened at the beginning of May, in New York, where spring arrived later. While he was looking out the window of his hotel room at the budding trees, becoming greener every day, he suddenly wanted to paint them—in watercolors. Back in London, his desire to use watercolors continued, starting with the view from his garden in Pembroke Studios, then, naturally, with Holland Park. It took him six months to master the technique. Watercolors forced him to work quickly and to anticipate the next five moves, as in playing chess, because you can't change anything. More than three layers and the colors lose their brightness. It was like painting and drawing at the same time. From landscapes he moved on to portraits. He did a series of thirty large double portraits, quickly, almost one a day, having his models pose in the same office chair, against the same light-green background. When the paintings were exhibited at the National Portrait Gallery, the critics found them unequal, clumsy, and caricatural. But he felt that by forcing him to paint quickly, by allowing an uninterrupted flow to come from his hand, watercolor had freed something in him. A process had been set in motion that was leading him somewhere, even if he didn't yet know where, as happened twenty years earlier when he had begun the photomontages. He just had to open himself up to it. For that, he had to return to Los Angeles, his place of work and inspiration for decades. In February 2003 he flew to California with John and pursued the watercolors in the studio on Montcalm Avenue. He was waiting.

He hadn't taken fate into account. In May, John went to London for a week to take care of some business; when he returned he was stopped at customs, questioned, held, then sent back to England. In the past, he had stretched the expiration date of his visa by a day or two; after 9/11 the immigration laws had become much stricter. David thought the ridiculous incident would only result in lost time and money. He called lawyers, collector friends who had contacts in the Bush administration, people in high places in his own country. He was one of the best-known living English painters, but the American bureaucrats didn't make any exceptions. Even if it was proven that John didn't represent a terrorist threat of any kind, he would not be allowed to return to the United States—to his home. David suddenly became aware of a reality that he hadn't experienced before: that of all the immigrants who were arrested daily and deported by force even though they had American children, a house, work. If they expelled his lover, they were expelling him too, because he couldn't live without John.

It was the country he had chosen. The country of freedom. Where was the California of his youth? After the Patriot Act, the Clean Indoor Air Act, which prohibited smoking in public places, had been enacted, reducing individual freedom a bit more. For your own good, said those health terrorists who had replaced tobacco with antidepressants and who held their noses as soon as they saw a cigarette, even extinguished, in the hand of a disgraceful old man. Picasso smoked and he died at ninety-one; Matisse smoked and he died at eighty-four; Monet smoked and he died at eighty-six; David's father, a militant antismoker, died at seventy-five. So...

He went back to England.

Because of the Patriot Act he had to leave the place that had been his source of inspiration for more than three decades. He couldn't even live where he wanted to. A painter, in this world, was nothing—just a rudderless ship tossed by the waves.

He settled for the summer in Yorkshire, in Bridlington, in the brick house near the beach that he had bought for his mother, to be close to his sister, Margaret, whose partner was very ill. After the man died, David stayed to keep Margaret company. Every day the brother and sister took long drives through the countryside and David felt particularly attracted to the Wolds, the low, undulating chalk hills of Yorkshire that he had known as a child. They ran into very few people, just a few farmers, no tourists, and Bridlington was far enough from London so that no one came to bother him. John, even more loving since David had left the States for him, joined him, as did the young French accordionist whom David had hired as an assistant on the recommendation of Ann and her husband. Jean-Pierre, whom they called JP, was no doubt the only Parisian in Bridlington. He served as David's chauffeur, driving him through the countryside in his car, stopping here and there so he could do a few sketches in a Japanese notebook that opened like an accordion. He grew to like even more that valley-filled landscape unsullied by any electric pole or billboard, and which they often drove through without seeing another car. In an hour and a half, he could fill an entire notebook with sketches of blades of grass. In drawing grass, he learned to see it—which he would never have been able to do taking photos—because when you draw it takes time to look and thus you become aware of space. Unlike the Yorkshire landscapes painted for Jonathan, his watercolors didn't represent the panoramic views or travels through the countryside, but cultivated fields along the road and the changing colors of the seasons.

Passing through Los Angeles in the spring of 2005, he suddenly wanted to paint oil portraits. After years with watercolors, this technique seemed so rich and so easy! Why deprive himself of it? Back in Bridlington, he started painting landscapes again, but with oils. There was no mistaking the energy and the joy that drove him. Since his strolls through Holland Park in April 2002, since he had been touched by grace—because that was exactly what it was: religious, spiritual grace—his subject was becoming clearer and clearer. He *was burning*, as is said in that game when a blindfolded child is getting closer to the goal. From farm fields he moved on to trees. A road bordered by trees, whose branches came together forming a natural arch, especially pleased him, and he painted it in each season, recording each variation of light and color. Nothing was as beautiful as the seasons. They were the very essence of change. Life.

He painted outside, from nature, like the painters of the Barbizon School in nineteenth-century France. In the winter, JP and he had to wear several layers of thick clothing that made them look like Michelin Men. In the summer, the light was most beautiful from six to nine in the morning, so they got up early. When it started to rain, JP opened a large umbrella, and the painting sometimes had traces of raindrops. David bought a Toyota pickup truck, a model used by soldiers in Afghanistan, which enabled them to take any path in any weather; they fitted it with wide shelves in the back so they could slide in the canvases when they weren't dry. He liked solving these concrete problems; they reminded him of activities at the scout camps of his youth. But above all, the more he painted the better he could see. And the better he could see, with more precision and intensity, the more he wanted to paint.

He had often noticed that moving from one continent to another entailed a change of perspective and brought new ideas. In Los Angeles, where he had gone for a retrospective of his portraits at LACMA in July 2006, he stuck reproductions of his landscapes up on the large wall of his studio. Each painting was made up of six juxtaposed canvases, and he put nine of them side by side. When he looked at them from a distance, he noticed that they seemed to form a single huge painting made of fifty-four canvases, and he wondered whether such a painting could be done. A painting that would measure more than twelve feet by forty feet. Gigantic, it would be almost twice as big as his biggest work, A Bigger Grand Canyon. The human eye couldn't handle such a voluminous work—but the computer, yes. His sister, who had a knack for computers, a year earlier had shown him how to scan his watercolors and email them to his friends in London and Los Angeles. The scanner was the solution to the problem. David could do a drawing by hand, divide it into rectangles of equal size, and scan it, creating a puzzle on the screen. He could then paint the parts one by one, without having to climb up on a ladder, all the while visualizing the whole.

He was euphoric when he returned to Bridlington. First, he had to find the right scene to paint. He looked for it while driving slowly with JP through the countryside. On the outskirts of a village called Warter, he saw a thicket of smaller trees around a very old, very big sycamore, as august as a patriarch. The branches of all those trees divided into a thousand smaller branches that were intertwined delicately, apparently not touching each other, all rising up to the sky. Those complex lines that resembled blood vessels or the convolutions of the brain went off in all directions, not following any rules of perspective.

He had found it. He was quite simply going to paint a tree. The painting would be almost as large as the tree in nature. The tree would be the heart of the painting—not the road, as in his canvases depicting his journeys. The tree was the hero. It humbly served humankind by releasing oxygen, by heating with its wood, and by providing shade. It incarnated the cycle of life by being covered in turn with buds, leaves, flowers, fruit, snow. No tree was like another. From observing them, David felt close to trees, as if they were his friends. Their twisted branches and knotty trunks reminded him of the arthritic hands of his mother, who, at the end of her life, could no longer even turn on a light. The trees were like his mother: patient, serene, rooted, devoted. They had a discreet, mysterious, and majestic presence.

He called the head curator of contemporary art at the Royal Academy and asked her to reserve the large wall at the back of Gallery III for him for the summer exhibition. Most of the hundred or so academicians hoped to hang their works there. The curator would have to persuade the exhibition committee and the Royal Academy's board. He had to convince her.

"I am going to create the largest plein air picture ever painted, Edith, and the largest painting ever shown in the 239 years of summer exhibitions at the Royal Academy."

His exaltation didn't come from the records he was going to break, but from the awareness that he was out to tackle his great work, finally. The painting would be mighty not only in size but also in what it portrayed. It would be the greatest painting of his whole career, the one up to which everything he'd ever done had been leading.

He had to hurry because there were only a few weeks left of winter, and in winter there were only six hours of light each day. He wanted to paint his tree in that season— when the branches, naked of the leaves that weighed on them and dragged them to the ground where we all end up, were alive. They rose up to the sky, light and free, and seemed to converse with it. Nothing was more elegant and more dignified than a tree in winter.

David wanted gallery visitors, when they walked into the room, to have a feeling of religious veneration, as in a cathedral. The painting should encompass the viewer, so that he would intuitively feel empathy with the work. That's why it needed to be so big. Its size would remind viewers of their smallness before immensity. He wanted to reproduce space, much more mysterious than the surface that a photo would show.

There was so much work that he had to have his former assistant come from Los Angeles to help. On-site he also hired an eighteen-year-old whom John had met at a barbecue and who sometimes walked their dogs to make a little pocket money. Then he rented a huge storage space in the industrial outskirts of Bridlington, where he could view his painting in its entirety.

Life was a puzzle in which, contrary to what he might have believed, nothing was left to chance. He was just beginning to understand how the pieces fit together. In the great book of nature, it was written that he would return to the land of his ancestors and of his childhood after decades in California in order to paint a tree that would be his great work. A series of circumstances as rigorous as a mathematical axiom had led him there: the new, very strict laws of American security that had forced John to return to England; his love for John, which had brought about his own return; his deafness, which enhanced his vision; the death of his mother; his sister's gift for computers; the detour through watercolors that had brought him closer to nature; the months he had spent posing for Lucian Freud while observing his slowness and precise eye; his daily crossing of Holland Park, whose spring transformation had enchanted him.

The painting that was exhibited at the Royal Academy was as impressive as he had hoped it would be, and the museum curator offered him the whole space of the museum for a large exhibition of his landscapes for 2012, the year of the Olympic Games in London. He had five years to prepare for it.

There was so much to see, so many variations in shapes and colors to record, that he hardly knew where to begin. Drops of rain falling in a puddle were enough to fascinate him. In the spring, the blooming of the hawthorns overwhelmed him. It lasted only two weeks, during which he could scarcely sleep: how could he miss even a moment of such a masterpiece? The most beautiful light was between five and six in the morning, so he left before sunrise. David and JP got up at five o'clock, like Monet at Giverny. From one day to the next, the bright green was magically transformed into white, and the white gradually covered the green entirely, a white made up of thousands of delicate flowers with the delicious scent of honey. There was an explosion of petals of such a creamy white that they brought to mind cream éclairs, and that's how he painted them, like a voluptuous thing that could be eaten—nature was transformed into a huge feast offered up to all the senses. In Japan, thousands of people drove to see the cherry trees in bloom; for the blooming of the hawthorns in Yorkshire he and JP were the only spectators. He spent two weeks painting nonstop and had to stay in bed afterward, because he had fallen ill, had contracted a high fever, without even realizing it. The following spring, he went even further:

the hawthorn bushes assumed a fantastical and almost anthropomorphic shape, leaning over the road as if they were going to devour the passerby.

He was seventy years old, soon seventy-one, and felt more alive than ever. "If the doors of perception were cleansed every thing would appear to man as it is, Infinite," wrote the poet William Blake. Old age was the cleansing of perception, the time when you wanted to snatch beauty from oblivion, a beauty you never saw better than when sexual desire and social ambition had faded. The Chinese said that painting was the art of old men, because their experience—of painting, of observation, of life—has accumulated throughout their lives and surges up in their works. David had finally discovered the infinity of the universe: not in the desert, not in the panoramic view from the north side of the Grand Canyon, or from on top of Garrowby Hill, but in the naked branches of trees, in a blade of grass, in the flowering of hawthorns. He no longer sought to dominate nature with his gaze; he had learned to look at it from below, humbly, and to blend into it by leaving his ego aside, as if to be swallowed by the hawthorn bushes. For the first time, it wasn't his work that enabled him to forget himself, but a contemplation of nature.

A painting in the Frick Collection in New York by Claude Lorrain, *The Sermon on the Mount*, with dark shading because it had been damaged in a fire, had caught David's attention. In it Jesus, on top of a little hill surrounded by his disciples, is talking to the shepherds below in the field, and the point of view is not from Jesus but from the shepherd and his wife in the foreground, who are contemplating the mountain in the middle of the canvas, the tiny Christ, and the huge sky, from below. The work accomplished that extraordinary feat: it attracted the gaze to the top and suspended the subject in the sky. David recognized his own new focal point. A high-resolution digital image of the painting the curator of the Frick gave him allowed him to restore it virtually and to retrieve its original colors, and he painted ten versions of it in a row, with increasingly bright, almost psychedelic colors. Once again, he had seized an ancient subject, renewed it, made it explode with color and life. Who painted religious scenes anymore?

He worked with the same frenzy that pushes someone to take drugs without being able to stop, except this was a creative frenzy, and it lasted for years without showing any signs of abating. Margaret had taught him how to use an iPhone. The Brushes app, which enabled you to draw on a screen with your thumb, gave him the same pleasure as that of a child finger painting. The iPhone offered an incomparable advantage early in the morning, when it was still too dark to draw without turning on the light, which would have destroyed the subtle nuances of tone seen in the rising sun. Each morning he sketched sunrises that he sent to his friends in London, New York, or Los Angeles. He was certain that Van Gogh would have sketched on an iPhone, if he had had one, the little drawings that dotted his letters to Theo, and that Rembrandt also would have used the technology if he had had access to it. When Steve Jobs announced the creation of the iPad a year later, David bought one immediately. The screen was four times bigger; he no longer drew with just his thumb, but with all his fingers or with a stylus. The device enabled him to immediately sketch everything that caught his eye—a glass ashtray filled with butts, a lamp and its reflection in the window, a faucet, his cap on a table, his foot next to his shoe when he got up in the morning, a bouquet of flowers. He had large pockets sewn into all his jackets so he would be able to bring his tablet everywhere, in any weather.

With the little high-definition cameras that JP attached to the sides of the Toyota, he filmed the transformations of nature from nine different angles along the same road, and created a work composed of a hypnotic multiplicity of screens that he called *The Four Seasons*. He would also choose not to use technology. He continued to paint trees, and dressed a large stump that looked like a totem pole, which he was getting attached to, in purple, like a bishop. He painted in bright colors the beautiful cut-down trees, transformed into logs piled up along the road, whose orange-hued slices resembled palpitating flesh. He made a huge painting of thirty-two canvases, a stylized depiction of the arrival of spring, that season when each plant, each bud, and each flower seemed to rise up, when all of nature was erect. The American critic Clement Greenberg had said that it was no longer possible to paint a landscape. He was going to put a genre that had fallen out of fashion since Constable and Turner back on the map.

Happiness didn't come from success, nor from the satisfaction of having achieved it against all odds, nor from the honors—shortly before his seventy-fifth birthday, the queen honored him with the Order of Merit, which at any one time can only be bestowed on at most twenty-four living people in all of the Commonwealth, and David accepted it even though he didn't care about medals, because he couldn't have refused without offending the queen. Nor did happiness come from money. His paintings were now selling for insane prices, and David had become very rich. But the fortune served only to provide a certain comfort and did not deliver what was essential, which was the desire to paint. Happiness came from working, of course, and from the awareness that the infinite was in the eye of the viewer. But above all, it came from friendship.

There was the circle of loyal friends who worked for him in Los Angeles and London—Gregory, Graves, and a few others—in whom he had absolute trust. There was the family circle: the brother and sister who still lived in Yorkshire, and with whom he had remained close over the years—Margaret, who lived near him and whom he saw almost every day, and Paul, who had retired and moved an hour away. And in Bridlington he had an intimate circle, which had finally chased away the specter of solitude. His team. A small number of close friends who shared his daily life in the brick house three minutes from the sea, who worried about him, who would never leave him.

Every day John bought flowers that he arranged artistically in various rooms of the house, walked their dogs, and cooked exquisite meals that he served in the dining room, whose walls were painted carmine red. He took care of them all like a mother. His room was on the second floor, at the other end of the hallway from David's. JP, who had become David's chief assistant, was like an adult and independent son. He lived in a studio on the ground floor, and on weekends often returned to London, where he had an apartment near the St Pancras train station. He still drove David through the countryside, and David felt blessed to have found such a patient ally, whose gaze had been heightened through the years and who was now as delighted at observing a landscape as David was. Another assistant spent a few days a week with them to take care of technical and computer matters. Then there was Dominic, Dom, the child of the house—the young man from Bridlington whom John had met at a barbecue when Dom was seventeen, and who had begun to work for David when he was painting his huge *Bigger Trees Near Warter*. Dom was now twenty-three, had left his university in his second year to work full time for David, and contributed his youthful energy and freshness to the team. His delight when David did his portrait, or when he gave him a key to the house, a sign of the confidence he had in him, reminded David of Byron's enthusiasm, even if physically the blond Dom with curly hair and athletic body didn't look anything like the dark and delicate Byron.

They were a family.

And they were more than that. They were a community of free spirits and bodies. In a world in which the individual was increasingly controlled by the media, the Internet, and the government, David had created an island of freedom. His Bridlington house was the last refuge of a bohemian life. They could smoke, drink, create all the artificial paradises they wanted, as long as they didn't harm anyone. By mutual agreement, John and David had ended their sexual relationship a few years earlier, when David turned seventy-one. John and Dominic had become lovers. Dom was twenty-five years younger than John; John was twenty-nine years younger than David. David could no longer drink or take hard drugs, or have an erection worthy of the name, but, far from feeling jealous, he was delighted at that transferal of desire under his roof. Tolerance was a virtue that was becoming extinct. The brick walls of the house with cantilevered windows three minutes from the sea sheltered a paradise.

It was a freedom that was difficult to preserve as one grew older. Age encloses you in rigid habits and instills in you all sorts of fears and neuroses. David had noticed this recently when he had had dinner with Peter and his partner in New York, for the first time in years. David's former lover was still living with the Danish fellow for whom he had left David, and the two men, ten years younger than he, no longer drank or smoked, couldn't stand the smell of cigarettes, ate only organic, and kept an eye on their watches so they wouldn't go to bed after 10 p.m.! You would have thought they were two old spinsters. After they said their goodbyes, David wondered how he could have been madly in love with that man.

He had been living in Bridlington for nine years. Nine years of ceaseless creativity. He had never had such a long cycle, even in California. Monet had lived forty-three years in his modest house in Giverny, with his cook, his gardener, his pond, and his wonderful studio: forty-three springs and forty-three summers. David couldn't imagine a better life. The office that took care of his business was in Los Angeles and opened at ten in the morning, 6 p.m. in Bridlington. He spent long, peaceful days, without any administrative concerns to disturb him. He worked without pause and felt no fatigue. One October morning, he went to get the newspaper, walking as usual along the vast beach that stretched toward the east, bordered by the white cliffs of Flamborough Head. While he was contemplating the gray expanse and the icy roiling of the North Sea, he smiled when he remembered what his sister had said: "Sometimes I think that space is God." It was an idea that was as true as it was poetic. He, too, felt happy only when he had space around him. He suddenly stumbled, for no reason—there wasn't a dip in the sand or a stone that had tripped him—and fell without hurting himself, then got up. After buying the newspaper, he went home and noticed that he couldn't finish his sentences. He made the connection between that sudden incapacity and his fall on the beach. John called an ambulance, which arrived in less than ten minutes. He had had a stroke. For the second time in his life John accompanied him to the hospital, holding his hand, in the ambulance this time.

It took David weeks, even months, to be able to talk normally again. He was aware of his luck: his right hand had been spared. That was more important than speech. It was his second attack, and it hadn't killed him any more than the first one had. Instead of pancreatic cancer like his friends Christopher, Henry, and Jonathan, he had suffered from a simple pancreatitis, which wasn't fatal. He had escaped the scourge of AIDS. Death was playing tricks on him, but at the end of the day those tricks merely reminding him that he was mortal. The time he had left to paint wasn't infinite.

After having used technology so much, he again wanted to go back to a traditional technique: charcoal. He began by drawing the stump that resembled a totem pole. Vandals had recently carved it into pieces and had covered it with graffiti. The profanation caused David a sadness that he expressed in his black-and-white drawings. Charcoal was perfect for depicting the nudity of winter, but he gave himself a challenge: to draw the arrival of spring in black and white, he who had forever loved strong, bright colors. Fatigued by his stroke and by the big landscape exhibition that had just taken place at the Royal Academy, which had been a huge popular and critical success, he went to bed at nine o'clock and got up later than before. In his car, sitting next to JP, who read or listened to music, he worked for hours, extremely concentrated. He had slowed down his rhythm, but life remained exciting at seventy-five, after two close calls with his health.

After spending the whole day outside with JP for the second consecutive day, he had only one desire: to close his eyes and sleep. Drawing demanded intense concentration and it exhausted his eye muscles. In his bedroom he took out his hearing aids and, barely lying down, fell into a sleep from which he emerged almost ten hours later. Coming into the kitchen in the morning, he saw JP sitting at the table, his head in his hands, in a pose that wasn't like him.

"You're already up, honey?"

JP raised his head. He had a strange expression on his face.

"David..."

He recognized the voice in a second. A white voice, metallic. He thought of John and was afraid.

"What happened?"

"Dom...Dom is dead."

"Dom?"

Impossible. He had seen him ten hours earlier in this very kitchen, when he had come to get a glass of water before going to bed. Dom, leaning in the open fridge door, wearing a T-shirt and underpants that showed his athletic thighs covered with fine blond hair, had started when he heard David come in, then turned around, an apple and a yogurt in his hands. Dom said he wouldn't be there Tuesday because he had to train for a rugby match.

David sat down. JP told him what had happened during the night. John and Dom had been on a drinking-and-drugs binge for the past two days. Dom had awakened John at four in the morning to ask him to drive him to the hospital. He was pale but didn't seem to be in pain and had been able to get dressed by himself, so John hadn't panicked. They left the house around five. On the way to the hospital, Dom passed out. They couldn't revive him. JP didn't know any more.

"Where is John?"

"At the hospital."

John returned home in a state of shock and had to be hospitalized a few days later. David and JP had seen the bottle of drain opener on the bathroom sink, empty, and had understood that Dom must have killed himself.

David forced himself to start drawing again. Only drawing took him out of himself. Art had that power. His eye concentrated on a blade of grass, the world disappeared. In May he drew every day, every new leaf, every new bud, every new petal, in black and white. Then he left for London with JP. He couldn't stay in Bridlington, a place haunted by memories of Dom, anymore.

It was the first death since his friend in Los Angeles. The first in twelve years, when he thought death had finally released its fangs. It was also the most horrible. Happening under his roof while he was sleeping. A child had killed himself next to him. He had seen nothing, heard nothing. It was the end of a life. The end of their team, their family, freedom, joy. The dark, morbid, moralistic world had won. At a time when the AIDS epidemic created a hecatomb among his friends, they were all victims. They didn't want to die. Now one of them, the youngest, had killed himself. The myopic nannies of England could rejoice. So could all the health terrorists on earth.

David and JP left for California. The Montcalm Avenue house hadn't changed, with its bright colors, nestled in tropical vegetation so green and so brilliant that it seemed to have been painted in acrylics. Nor had California changed; it was still just as luminous, fragrant, and sunny. There was the same vast blue sky, indifferent to tragedies. It felt good to wake up in the morning and feel the heat on his skin, go down the Prussian-blue stairs to the pool sparkling under the sun in the middle of palm trees, fuchsias, agaves, and aloes. David didn't leave the house and saw no one. He couldn't paint anymore.

Sitting on the wooden terrace with the Prussian-blue balustrade, he saw Dom in front of the refrigerator and the expression of surprise on his child's face when he turned around and noticed David at the entrance to the kitchen. He heard Dom tell him that he wouldn't be there Tuesday because he was training for a match. He played over and over in his head the scene he hadn't witnessed. Dom waking up in the middle of the night in John's bed, going to the bathroom, taking the plastic bottle from under the toilet, pressing the top on each side with two fingers while pushing and turning it. That safety cap that protected children from accidentally ingesting the dangerous liquid was like an ad for mortal danger. Dom ignored it. He had brought the bottle to his lips and tilted it up. Drank, like water or whiskey, the sulfuric acid that served to unclog pipes. Dom drank his death the way Socrates drank the cup of hemlock. Hadn't the pale yellow liquid burned his lips, his throat, and his esophagus right away? When he had gone into the bathroom was it to piss or to kill himself? Had the bottle of drain opener given him the idea, the way the void attracts someone with vertigo? Had he regretted his act in the second that followed it? Apparently, since he woke up John to take him to the hospital. That idea horrified David. There was no turning back. Even if John had called 911, they couldn't have saved him. The acid had already done its work. Did the loss of consciousness come before the pain, as David hoped?

Why had death been content to brush by him only to strike down a twenty-three-year-old next to him? Why had Dom been sacrificed? Questions kept spinning in his head.

One day he saw JP sitting in a yellow chair with wooden arms, his head in his hands, in the exact position David had found him when he entered the Bridlington kitchen five months earlier. He suddenly felt like painting him. He asked him not to move, went to get his sketchbook, and got to work.

He now wanted friends or acquaintances to come over so he could do their portraits, sitting in the same yellow chair with wooden arms, against the same blue-green background, even brighter than in the watercolors he had done ten years earlier, before his landscapes. He didn't paint them with their heads in their hands, like JP. He painted their faces looking at him. While he worked, he managed not to think of Dom. Rather, thinking of Dom was transmuted into lines, strokes, colors. These portraits of the living didn't cover up the dead; they were his tomb.

He was once again engaged in life. Capable of drawing and painting the living. Able to prepare the big exhibition that was opening at the de Young Museum in San Francisco in October, and the many others that would take place in galleries in London, New York, Los Angeles, Paris,

Beijing... Able to say to the journalist who had come to interview him, to the filmmaker who came to film him for a documentary: "I am an optimist." He was seventy-nine. His deafness prevented him from having a normal social life: as soon as there were more than three people in a room he couldn't hear a thing. He no longer left his house except to go to the dentist, the doctor, the bookstore, or a marijuana dispensary. He had been given a card for medical marijuana, to calm his anxiety—the anxiety of no longer having access to marijuana, he thought, smiling. In a year there would be a major retrospective at the Tate, which would then travel to Paris, to the Centre Pompidou, then to the Metropolitan Museum of New York. It would be a journey through six decades of his work. Preparation for such an event involved enormous work. The Montcalm Avenue studio was again transformed into a hive of activity. David spent his days there with his assistants, busier than ever.

He contemplated his most recent work while smoking his legally obtained joint. Inspired by two paintings, one by Caravaggio and the other by Cézanne, the drawing done on the iPad that he had then printed out represented three men of mature age playing cards. He had placed under that image the three screens on which he had created the portraits of those men, and activated a function of the iPad that enabled him to replay at high speed the execution of the drawing from the first stroke to its completion. David, like the spectator who would soon look at that work, saw himself drawing in an accelerated mode. Each stroke was made quickly, a face appeared, the hand changed direction, erased, turned the face in another direction, changed its expression. The work hanging on the wall opposite him represented at the same time the completed drawing and the movement of creation: it was perfectly consistent with his whole work, and it was something new he had created at the age of seventy-nine. Tomorrow he would undertake another project: three men smoking. Tobacco or marijuana? There wouldn't be any smell to betray them. A bit of propaganda wouldn't hurt. A new idea was already taking shape: to paint an Annunciation in the style of Piero della Francesca. A Californian Annunciation with psychedelic colors, like his *Sermon on the Mount* after Claude Lorrain. To celebrate birth, love, the cycle of life, in an explosion of color. After the dark charcoal landscapes of England, this return to California was a return to the brightest and most audacious of colors.

Portraits after landscapes. Spring after winter. The hand after technology. Oil after watercolors. Color after charcoal. California after England. Joy after tragedy. The dawn after night. Creation after the void. And so on. Everything occurred in alternation. There were no answers to useless questions. Just cycles. Life wasn't a straight road with a linear perspective. Winding, it stopped, started again, reversed, then leapt forward. Chance, tragedy, were part of the great design. The great design, drawing, weren't they the same thing? The ability to perceive order in the chaos of the world. That is what attracted David to art, what he liked best in his favorite painters, Piero della Francesca or Claude Lorrain: the complex balance of colors and opposed elements, the place of man in space, the feeling that he was but a small part of a greater whole. The artist was the priest of the universe.

There was only one certainty: the child, as soon as he could hold a pencil, made a mark. Since the beginning of time, humans have attempted to express in two dimensions their wonder before a three-dimensional world. That would not stop anytime soon.

ACKNOWLEDGMENTS

I wish to thank the following people for their wonderful encouragement and useful comments: Luciana Floris, Mylène Abribat, Charles Kermarec, Hélène Landemore, Ben Lieberman, Mirjana Ciric, Gordana de la Roncière, Hilari Allred, Jacqueline Letzter, Wadie Sanbar, Hilary Reyl, Rosine Cusset, Amanda Filipacchi, Richard Hine, Alessandro Ricciarelli, Jennifer Cohen, Shelley Griffin, Catherine Texier, Denis Hollier, Nathalie Bailleux, and Anne Vijoux.

I also thank my editor, Jean-Marie Laclavetine, and Antoine Gallimard for their unwavering support, as well as my American publisher, Judith Gurewich, my editor, Alexandra Poreda, and the whole team at Other Press, for welcoming this little book.

SELECT BIBLIOGRAPHY

Works are given in order of importance for this novel.

BOOKS

David Hockney. *David Hockney*. London: Thames and Hudson, 1976.

David Hockney. *That's the Way I See It*. London: Thames and Hudson, 1993.

David Hockney. *Secret Knowledge: Rediscovering the Lost Techniques of the Old Masters*. London: Thames and Hudson, 2006.

Christopher Simon Sykes. *David Hockney: A Rake's Progress. The Biography, 1937–1975*. New York: Doubleday, 2012.

Christopher Simon Sykes. *David Hockney: A Pilgrim's Progress. The Biography, 1975–2012*. New York: Doubleday, 2014.

Lawrence Weschler. *True to Life: Twenty-Five Years of Conversations with David Hockney*. Berkeley: University of California Press, 2008.

Martin Gayford. *A Bigger Message: Conversations with David Hockney.* London: Thames and Hudson, 2011.

George Rowley. *Principles of Chinese Painting.* Princeton: Princeton University Press, 1947.

Marco Livingstone and Kay Haymer. *Hockney's Portraits and People.* London: Thames and Hudson, 2003.

Tim Barringer et al. *David Hockney: A Bigger Picture.* London: Royal Academy of Arts, 2012.

Richard Benefield, Lawrence Weschler, Sarah Howgate, and Gregory Evans. *David Hockney: A Bigger Exhibition.* San Francisco: Fine Arts Museums of San Francisco, 2013.

Didier Ottinger, editor. *David Hockney: Catalogue officiel de l'exposition, Paris, Centre Pompidou, du 21 juin au 23 octobre 2017.* Paris: Centre Pompidou, 2017.

ARTICLES

Peter Fuller. "An interview with David Hockney." *Art Monthly*, no. 12 (November 1977): 4–10.

Hilton Kramer. "The Fun of David Hockney." *New York Times*, November 4, 1977.

Nigel Bunyan. "David Hockney assistant died after drinking drain cleaner, inquest told." *Guardian*, August 29, 2013.

Simon Hattenstone. "David Hockney: 'Just because I'm cheeky, doesn't mean I'm not serious.'" *Guardian*, May 9, 2015.

FILMS

Philip Haas and David Hockney. *A Day on the Grand Canal with the Emperor of China, or: Surface Is Illusion But So Is Depth*. 46 minutes. 1988.

Jack Hazan. *A Bigger Splash*. Starring David Hockney. 106 minutes. 1974.

Randall Wright. *Hockney*. 112 minutes. 2014.

Monique Lajournade and Pierre Saint-Jean. *David Hockney: In Perspective*. 52 minutes. 1999.

CATHERINE CUSSET was born in Paris in 1963. A graduate of the École normale supérieure in Paris and *agrégée* in Classics, she taught eighteenth-century French literature at Yale from 1991 to 2002. She is the author of thirteen novels, including *The Story of Jane* and *L'autre qu'on adorait* (short-listed for the 2016 Prix Goncourt), and has been translated into seventeen languages. Cusset lives in Manhattan with her American husband and daughter.

TERESA LAVENDER FAGAN is a freelance translator. She has published more than a dozen book-length translations, including Jean Bottéro's *The Oldest Cuisine in the World: Cooking in Mesopotamia* and Yannick Haenel's *Hold Fast Your Crown*.